PEGGY GOODY

Peggy Goody

The Black Eagle School for Wizards

Book 4

Charles S Hudson

Order this book online at www.trafford.com
or email orders@trafford.com

Most Trafford titles are also available at major online book retailers.

Print information available on the last page.

ISBN: 978-1-4907-5758-2 (sc)
ISBN: 978-1-4907-5757-5 (e)

Trafford rev. 04/15/2015

Trafford www.trafford.com
PUBLISHING

North America & international
toll-free: 1 888 232 4444 (USA & Canada)
fax: 812 355 4082

CONTENTS

Chapter 1 – The Journey Begins 1

Chapter 2 – A Surprise Attack 4

Chapter 3 – The Snake 11

Chapter 4 – The Black Eagle School 16

Chapter 5 – A Close Call 19

Chapter 6 – The Den 24

Chapter 7 – The Tour 28

Chapter 8 – The Report 36

Chapter 9 – Savajic Arrives 38

Chapter 10 – The Enemy Within 40

Chapter 11 – Lockstay Prison 43

Chapter 12 – The Hide 46

Chapter 13 – The Plan 49

Chapter 14 – The Revelation 52

Chapter 15 – The Search 55

Chapter 16 – Wizard History 58

Chapter 17 – The Bridge 62

Chapter 18 – Battell Crie 67

Chapter 19 – Surf Polo 69

Chapter 20 – Animal Instinct... 72

Chapter 21 – The Gift... 77

Chapter 22 – Fu-Jin-Mojo 86

Chapter 23 – Bad News from America... 89

Chapter 24 – Love Is In The Air 93

Chapter 25 – A letter from Kate 95

Chapter 26 – Polo + the Screamers 97

Chapter 27 – The Decision... 99

Chapter 28 – Time To Say Good-Bye 102

Chapter 1

THE JOURNEY BEGINS

A t last, the day Peggy had been waiting for had arrived. Henry had come to pick her up and take her to Savajic's home. She was to stay there overnight and prepare herself for her first day at the Black Eagle School for Wizards.

Peggy hugged her mother and said good-bye. As she walked towards the car, Rose called out to her. She turned and Rose shouted, "I love you!" and blew her a kiss, and Peggy blew one back to her.

The car drove silently away from the cottage and disappeared into the sky. A few minutes later it landed on the drive at Savajic's home. It made its way smoothly up to the front steps, where both Savajic and Owen were waiting to greet her. As soon as Peggy got out of the car, Owen rushed over to her and hugged her.

"I've really missed you," he said.

"And so have I," said the rich voice of Savajic.

Peggy turned to Savajic and smiled. "I've missed you too," she said. "It really is great to be back."

They walked up the stone steps and through the Great Hall to the back terrace. Cooper had laid the table with tea and biscuits, and when they had all sat down he began to pour the tea; they all had milk, but no sugar.

"Will that be all?" enquired Cooper.

"Yes. thank you, Cooper," replied Savajic, and Cooper retired back into the house.

Savajic looked at Peggy. "Have you any concerns about tomorrow?" he asked. "Because I do realise that it must feel quite daunting for you to be entering into a new school with a different type of culture and very different ideas."

Peggy smiled. "I am a little bit nervous, to be honest, but I have Owen to look after me and show me around. And besides, Lilly and Charlie will be there, so I probably already have more real friends than most of the students." She gave Owen and Savajic a big smile and said, "You know, I feel better already."

Savajic said, "For today, Peggy, I have asked Owen if he will run through the various school rules and regulations with you that you will have to abide by at Black Eagle. You will find everything that you need for your classwork, from books to pens, laid out in your room. And one last thing; may I also suggest that you try on your robe, just in case it needs any final adjustments."

Peggy sat quietly sipping her tea; how she loved it here! It really felt like home. It was a magical place, warm and welcoming. She almost felt guilty just having such thoughts; after all, the cottage was her home, and she loved her mother more than anything. But then again, she also remembered how much her mother had loved her stay here. She finished her tea and said to Owen, "I'm ready if you are; shall we get started?"

Owen had it all planed. "It's a lovely day, so I've taken the liberty of putting up a picnic basket, and I've asked Jenkins to saddle the horses and get them ready for us. And I thought that we could go over everything while we have a picnic."

Peggy was impressed. "What a lovely thought," she said. "Let me get changed and we can get started."

She was changed and back down on the terrace in no time at all. "I'm ready," she said, beaming at Owen.

"Great," said Owen. "Let's go." They walked across the terrace and down the stone steps hand in hand, chatting away to each other without a care in the world. When they arrived at the stables, Jenkins was waiting for them with their horses saddled and ready to ride. Then, after wishing each other good morning, they mounted their horses and rode off.

Down by the far end of the lake was a big old oak tree; it had a bench seat that circled its massive trunk. Owen decided that it was the perfect spot for him to go over the school rules and regulations with her, and then they could relax and enjoy their picnic. He had brought a folder with all kinds of information about the school, and as soon as Peggy was comfortable, he started to go through it with her. quite a few of the rules were the same as St. Ann's, but some of them sounded really strange to her; they referred to Spell Fields, Surf Polo Fields, The Grande Rock Faces, Forbidden Libraries, Creature Zoo, Telescope Dome, and many more strange-sounding places.

Peggy sighed. She said, "I'll never remember all this, Owen."

"You will do when you get there and see it. most of it will seem obvious to you.

"How do we get there tomorrow? Will Henry take us?"

Owen smiled. "It's not that simple," he said. "He will take us as far as the Boarding Station. It's a meeting place for all the wizards that are going to The Black Eagle School for Wizards. From there we get a bendy bus; we call it The Snake. It holds all the wizards. This will take us directly to the school. If you are not on the bus, you will not be allowed into the school, unless you have the personal permission from the headmaster, Professor Ableman. It's a safety precaution, designed to stop anyone getting into the school who is not invited."

"I'm so excited," said Peggy. "I can't wait for tomorrow to come."

Owen opened up the picnic basket and laid out the food on the bench. "I don't know about you, but I'm starving," he said, biting into a sandwich, and Peggy followed suit.

They sat there chatting about everything, from their first meeting at the cottage, right up until the present moment. "We'll see Lilly and Charlie at the boarding station," said Owen.

"I can't wait," said Peggy. "And don't forget, Owen, you've got something to tell Lilly."

"Don't get started on that again," he said. "I'll do it in my own time." They both started to laugh.

Chapter 2

A SURPRISE ATTACK

Bang! A shot rang out, bark splintered from off the trunk of the tree. *Bang! Bang!* Peggy felt a red-hot pain in her leg, and blood was running down her face from a graze on her head. Owen's wand was out and pointing at Peggy. "Proti!" he screamed at the top of his voice. The bubble was over Peggy just in time, as a hail of bullets hit the shield and bounced off.

Owen was hiding behind Peggy's shield. he needed to move around, so he couldn't afford to put himself into a protection bubble. He held out his wand, pointing it in front of Peggy. "Parto!" he commanded and immediately, a façade of the oak tree appeared ten metres in front, blocking off the view of the shooter. He waited until the shooting had stopped, then removed the bubble from Peggy. She was bleeding, and in pain.

Owen pointed his wand at Peggy. "Levita!" Peggy rose into the air. "Proti!" Owen guided Peggy gently into the saddle of her horse. He knew that once there she couldn't fall off. "Can you hear me, Peggy?"

"Yes," came the answer.

"Listen carefully; I want you to concentrate and Haze until you are safely back at the house." Peggy slowly disappeared. "Home!" he commanded, and the horse galloped off towards the house. Owen waited a few minutes to make sure that Peggy was well out of sight, and then he removed the façade. He didn't wait around to give the shooter another target. He jumped up onto his horse and followed Peggy home.

The horse came to a halt by the terrace, and Peggy came out of her Haze. Savajic rushed down the steps. He could see that Peggy was in pain and bleeding. He gathered her up in his arms and made straight for his workshop.

"Open!" he commanded as he approached, and the door sprung open. He gently laid her down on his bench. She had a deep graze on her head, and a bullet was lodged in her thigh. He took the bottle of green liquid from his glass cabinet and placed it on the bench beside her, then he took out his wand and pointed it down over the hole in Peggy's leg. He closed his eyes and slowly lifted his wand, and as he did, the bullet rose up from out of Peggy's thigh. He lowered his wand and put it down on the bench, then he picked up the bottle of green liquid and poured some into the palm of his hand, gently smoothing it onto the wound. a green haze covered her leg and when it cleared, the wound had disappeared. Then he did the same to Peggy's head wound, and within minutes, Peggy was back to normal, and looking as if nothing had happened.

She sat up just as Owen came rushing through the door. "Is she all right, Father?"

"Look for yourself," said Savajic.

Peggy sat there smiling at him and said, "You saved my life, Owen. Thank you."

Owen sat down in Savajic's chair with a thump, and let out a massive sigh of relief. He looked up at Savajic and said, "Thank you, Father."

Savajic gave Peggy a concerned look. "We will need to talk," he said. "But first, have a shower and change your clothes. I'll meet you on the terrace in an hour." Then he turned to Owen. "Let us take tea, and tell me in detail everything that has happened."

Owen explained how he and Peggy had chosen to stop by the large oak tree at the far end of the lake. He said that they had spent about an hour going through the rules and regulations of Black Eagle, and had then started eating their picnic. They had more or less finished eating when they had come under fire.

He told him how they had been caught by surprise and unfortunately, Peggy had been hit twice before he could put a protective bubble over her. Then he explained how he had put up a façade, removed the bubble from off Peggy, and put her onto her horse and sent her home. He had waited for a few minutes, then removed the façade and rode home.

"Do you think that Demodus is behind all of this?" Owen asked.

Savajic had been listening carefully to every detail of Owen's account of what had taken place. "Before I answer your question, Owen," he said, "please let me ask you something else. When you were sitting with Peggy, in which direction were you facing?"

"We were facing towards the forest," replied Owen.

"So you yourself were in full view if someone was looking out from the forest?"

"Well, yes," said Owen.

"And Peggy was not shielding you in any way?"

"No, she wasn't."

"Then that leads me to the conclusion that Peggy was specifically targeted. This makes me think that it is unlikely that Demodus was behind this attack. I'm afraid it is much more complicated. I believe that the attack has come from someone in the wizard world. I also feel that someone has alerted the Black Watch of Peggy's powers, and it is of great concern to them. So much so that it has forced them into making this murderous attack on her. I also believe that the attack was mounted in such a way as to make us think that it was the work of Demodus.

"If you recall your run-in with the Demodoms, they were shooting at a moving target with Peggy, and they only got one shot off before she Hazed. By the time that they had turned their attention to you, you were already under a Proti bubble.

"We have their weapons down in my workshop, and you will recall that they have telescopic sights. If it had been the Demodoms, I believe that both of you would have been killed. This shooting was meant to kill Peggy alone, but its planning was sloppy and rushed. As you know, wizards have no use for guns. whoever did the shooting couldn't have had much time to practice."

When Peggy came back down to the terrace she seemed to be quite relaxed. considering what she had just experienced, it was amazing. Savajic told her what he had concluded from Owen's account. "It seems to me that someone close to us has informed the

Black Watch Movement that you have become a wizard, and of the magic that you have learned. It has made them very uneasy, and worried enough to try to murder you.

"There are only two people apart from us here that know of Peggy's whereabouts and what she has been doing here, and they are Lilly and Charlie. I know that it seems unthinkable that one of them would betray us, but we have to be practical, and think this thing through logically. I personally can't remember asking either Lilly or Charlie *not* to talk about Peggy before they had left for home. It only needed for one of them—or both, for that matter—when they were in Wizard Company to say that Peggy was the fastest wizard that they had ever seen. Word would spread like wildfire to other wizards.

"I know that as soon as they got home from here, they intended to meet up later with some of the polo team and go to a surfing show, so they could easily have let it out there without thinking that it could do any harm. Remember, the Black Watch Movement have spies everywhere.

"Now, Peggy, while you are in this house, nothing can harm you. Once you are inside the Black Eagle School you will be safe. But from now on, Peggy, you and Owen must stay alert, and you must tell Lilly and Charlie what has happened at the first opportunity you get. Because the attacks will not end here, and if whoever is behind this finds out about your oath of allegiance, all four of you could become targets."

Peggy sat quite still, taking in what Savajic had just said to them. At last the penny had dropped, and she realised that this wasn't a game. Instinctively her hand went up and stroked the side of her head. Her bright green eyes were wide open, and her whole body shook in an ice-cold shiver. She knew that she had survived a bullet that had only been an inch away from killing her. If it hadn't been for the lightning actions of Owen and his skill at weaving spells, and the healing skills of Savajic, she would not be sitting there now.

Savajic watched her; he knew what she was going through. When he was a young man, two years after graduating from Black Eagle, he and his father had stood back to back in a stable yard. His father had taken him there to buy him a horse for his birthday. Five hooded wizards, members of the Black Watch Movement known as the Death Riders had tracked them there, and trapped them. "Make a last wish,

Andric, before you die," one of them had said to his father. They were the last words that he would ever say.

Savajic had showed them all that day why he was a speed champion. In a lightning-fast move his wand was out, and three of the wizards fell to the floor, dead. His father had killed one, and they both hit the fifth one together. After that day, his life was never quite the same; his fooling around had stopped. He had suddenly grown into a man, all in that one moment in time, and now he knew that Peggy was experiencing one such moment.

Peggy looked at Owen and Savajic in turn; she hesitated for a moment, and said to Savajic, "What would have happened if they had been trying to kill Owen?"

"What do you mean?" he replied.

"Well, I couldn't have saved him like he saved me. I wouldn't have known how."

"Why not, Peggy? Can you cast a Proti spell?"

"Yes."

"Can you cast a Parto spell?"

"Yes."

"And how about a Levita and a Pulshe spell?"

"Well, yes," she said.

"Then why couldn't you save Owen? They are the very spells that he used to save you, so you see, there is no reason for you to think otherwise. It would be unfair of us to expect you to grasp the many uses and situations where you could or would use the spells. And so what we do now is to make absolutely sure that you have mastered them all, and with your super speed you will be a match for anyone.

"I never anticipated that you would come under attack so soon, which means that I, too, have to be more vigilant. I should have realised that the Black Watch Movement have their spies everywhere, and now the Death Riders seem to have raised their evil heads again. They will show no mercy to anyone, and they will be a constant threat.

"The good news, however, is that once you are at Black Eagle, you will be tutored by Professor Battell Crie; he is Professor for Strategy and Defence against the Evil Arts. He has been given instructions from Enzebadier Abel that he is to take you under his wing and give you intensive one-to-one lessons.

"As for now, you have the power and speed to defeat most wizards. The Flecta spell will give you this. remember that you beat Owen on the range, and he is the current speed champion, so you have no reason to be afraid. remember this; suspect everyone, trust no one, and be prepared at all times.

"Now, about your robes," said Savajic, suddenly changing the subject. "Can you go and change into them and come down and perhaps give us a twirl?"

"Of course," said Peggy, and she headed off towards her room. As soon as she was in her room she undressed and laid her clothes on the bed, then she commanded, "School Robes." Instantly her clothes disappeared and her robes appeared in their place. She took her dress and put it on, and as she expected, it was a perfect fit. Her dress and cloak were black, a standard colour for the school. the only difference was their "House" colours; the braid around her cloak and its silk lining were bright crimson red, as were the inside of the pleats in her dress.

She stood in front of the large mirror that stood in the corner of her room, and as she twirled around, the crimson-red pleats in her dress opened up and looked like a ring of fire. She stopped and put on her cloak, and again it was a perfect fit. her loose-fitting hood hung down behind her and exposed the rich, crimson-red silk lining, and her long blonde hair hung down over her shoulders. she looked stunning.

As she walked onto the terrace, Savajic stood up and applauded her. "Brava!" he shouted. "A true wizard if ever I saw one."

Owen joined in. "Yes!" he shouted.

Peggy's cheeks were as red as the inside of her cloak. "Thank you," she said, and stood there feeling a little awkward.

Savajic broke the silence. "Why don't you both go down to the pool and relax before we have dinner this evening? Remember, it will be some time before we are all together again after tonight."

"Great idea," said Owen. "Come on, Peggy, let's get changed, and I'll see you down there."

They passed a few pleasant hours together, swimming and sitting around talking about school and things, and then they decided to have some time alone in their rooms. Peggy wanted to talk to her mother, and Owen had things to organize for the surf polo team.

Dinner was a pleasant enough affair, with most of the time being spent talking about Black Eagle. but there was no doubt that all three of them wanted to see the end of this day. And as they wished each other good night and retired to their rooms, there seemed to be just a touch of relief in the air.

When Peggy got back to her room, she had a shower and got into bed. She sat up, looking at her mother's face in her belt buckle. How she loved her! She recalled her mother's reaction when she had told her that she had mixed blood with Savajic and became a wizard. She could hear her mother's angry voice. She now realised what she had meant about power and danger going together hand in hand, and the greater the power, the greater the danger. She alone had made the choice to enter a world of magic and shadows, and she intended to play her part to the best of her ability.

Next morning, breakfast was so different; there was a definite sense of excitement. Today was the big day for Peggy, and Owen was just as excited; he had Lilly on his mind, and couldn't wait to see her again. As soon as breakfast was over, Peggy and Owen went to change into their robes. When they came back down, Henry was waiting for them in the Great Hall. They both had their school cases and their surf boards.

"Are you ready, Master Owen?" Henry asked.

"Yes," came the answer from both of them.

When they got down to the car, Savajic was waiting for them. He shook hands with Owen and whispered, "Look after Peggy for me, son."

"I will," Owen assured him.

Then when Savajic turned to Peggy, she threw her arms around him and kissed him on the cheek. "Thank you for everything!" she gushed.

Savajic smiled at her and said, "Make your mother and me proud of you; that is all that we could wish for. Now I will say good-bye. remember to keep your wand close to you at all times, and be vigilant." The car slid smoothly down the drive and took to the sky.

Chapter 3
THE SNAKE

I n what seemed to be only minutes, the car had stopped, and Peggy noticed that they were still in the sky. "Jump out!" said Owen.

"But we're still up in the sky!" she said.

Owen laughed, "I told you that things would be different. just wait until you open the door."

"Well, if you say so," said Peggy, and pushed open the door.

The sound of hundreds of voices all speaking at the same time hit her; it was unbelievable. They were on what looked like a massive bus depot, with wizards everywhere, all chattering away excitedly. She stepped out, and Owen followed her. he closed the door behind him and the car disappeared.

"Peggy!" It was the unmistakable Australian twang of Charlie's voice. He ran towards her and grabbed her in his strong arms and swung her round and round. "How are ya, mate?" he said.

"tip top," she said, mimicking his accent. He put her down and they stood there laughing. He looked at her and said, "Ya know, I've really missed ya, sport."

"And I've missed you, too," said Peggy.

"Really? That's great," said Charlie.

Owen was looking around anxiously. "Have you seen Lilly anywhere, Charlie?" he asked.

"No, she hasn't got here yet," he replied. "Can't wait to see her."

"Neither can I," said Owen.

"Hello!" They spun around; it was Lilly. she looked beautiful, and her long, blue-black hair was woven into a magnificent French plait that hung down across the red silk lining of her hood.

"Wow!" said Charlie. "You look great!" and gave her a bear hug.

"Let me go, you big lump," she said. "You don't know your own strength."

"OK," said Charlie, and pretended to wipe a tear from his eye, and that made them all laugh.

"This one will never change," said Owen, putting his arm around Charlie. Then he looked at Lilly. "How are you?" he asked her.

"I'm good." said Lilly. "And you?"

"Never felt better," he replied.

"Come on," said Charlie. "Let's mingle, and I'll show you what a crazy bunch of wizards you're going to get mixed up with." He grabbed Peggy's hand and pulled her towards a group of six wizards all huddled together. "Hi-ya, guys!" he shouted at them as they got closer.

"Hello, Charlie!" they shouted back in chorus.

"Who's your friend, Charlie?" asked a tall, handsome and suntanned wizard.

"Put your eyes back in," said Charlie, and turning to Peggy said, "This is Sal Mendez. Latin lover from Brazil, and the scourge of all the ladies. He is one of our surf polo team."

Sal took Peggy's hand and kissed it on the back. "The pleasure, I assure you, is all mine," he said, and he gave her a smile that exposed a perfect set of dazzling white teeth.

"Please, Peggy, let me introduce you to the rest of the team; this is Singh Machul and his sister, Fatima. They're from India." They smiled at Peggy and said hello.

"And this is Kate Stringer from the USA."

"Hi, Peggy," she said, shaking her hand with a firm grip.

"And this is our rock, Angus Fume. He's from Scotland." He nodded his head and said hello.

"And last but not least, from Germany is Helda Scelda, our top scorer and school swimming champion."

"Pleased to meet you, Peggy," she said.

Kate was the first to speak. "How come we've never seen you here before, Peggy?"

Charlie interrupted, "It's a long story, Kate, but you guys will be the first to know, I promise."

Kate was from Texas, and was not one to beat around the bush. She lived with her father on a magnificent ranch that bred racehorses. Her mother had died two years before, and Kate had become very close to her father. He had sent her to Black Eagle to learn as much magic as possible, and how to use it. The USA had only four wizards still living, and two of them were extremely old; they both lived in New York, and neither one had descendants. The Wizard War had taken a terrible toll on the USA wizards, and whole bloodlines had disappeared forever. This made Kate very special. Being an only child, she would in time become the last wizard in the USA, unless she married and had children of her own.

Helda spoke next. "Can you swim, Peggy?"

"Yes," said Peggy.

"Are you any good?"

"I think so," said Peggy. "Why?"

"I could really use a good, reliable swimmer on my team; we need to give White Eagle a good thrashing this year."

Angus butted in, "Come on, Helda, give the lass a chance to settle in." He had a deep, strong, and warm voice. then out of the blue he said, "Peggy, would you do me the honour of letting me show you around Black Eagle and its grounds? That is, of course, after you've settled in."

Peggy looked at him in surprise. "Oh! Yes, please, that would be lovely," she said. "Thank you."

Angus was beaming. "I've got my first date booked already," he said, looking straight at Sal Mendez. Sal turned away, pretending to be jealous.

"You've lost your touch, Sal," mocked Charlie.

Sal turned around with a wicked grin on his face. "I don't want you to worry, Peggy, but when Angus gets you lost, I'll come and show you the way home." They all burst out laughing.

Last term, Angus had been asked by Professor Grimlook, keeper of the Creature Zoo, to go to the zoo and bring back a Slick Back Grelch, a creature with the body of a mole and the head of a lizard.

Charlie and Sal had followed him to the zoo, and when Angus had gone into the cage, they locked him in and ran away. It had taken two hours to find him, with the whole of Redgrave looking for him, and from then on he had been teased about getting lost.

Suddenly, from out of nowhere, a horn blew out a loud tune and the bendy bus appeared. "Come on!" shouted Charlie. "Let's all get on a table together!" When Peggy stepped onto the bus she couldn't believe her eyes. From the outside it looked like a normal bus, but inside it was vast, with tables of food and drinks, and surrounded by round tables and chairs for them all to sit and eat. Charlie had moved onto a table that was big enough for all of them. "Let's get something to eat," he said. "I'm starving."

The food was wonderful. Every cake, sandwich, and savoury that you could think of was there, and the drinks were just as good. They each took a plate and filled it with whatever they wanted, then sat down at the table. "Make sure you eat plenty, Peggy," Charlie said. "It's the last meal we get until this evening."

As everyone settled down to their meal, the bendy bus pulled smoothly away, and a cheer went up that was so loud it was deafening. Then the chattering started. everyone was so excited, they all seemed to be talking at once. Peggy recalled how excited Cindy and she used to be on their first day back at school, but this time it was different; a different school, and different friends.

"Peggy, you are very quiet," said a soft voice. It was Fatima Machul.

"I'm sorry," said Peggy. "I was daydreaming."

"Yes, I remember when Singh and I first came here. We were totally bewildered. Everything is so different to our home in India, so I can imagine how you feel. But we soon made friends, and last year we both made the surf polo team. Now everybody knows who we are."

Peggy thought how much she reminded her of Cindy; the long, shiny black hair and beautiful face. She was certain even then that they would become close friends.

"How about you, Peggy?" asked Kate. "You're obviously English, but how come we've never seen you here before?"

Before she could answer, Owen butted in. "Kate, it's a long story, and I propose that we tell the six of you later tonight when we've settled in and had dinner. We'll meet up in the Redgrave den, is that OK?" They all nodded in agreement. The talk changed to last year's surf polo games and how they scored in different games, but the big game last year was when they beat the White Eagle champions; and now it was their last year at Black Eagle. They wanted to leave as champions.

A deafening cheer went up again; the driver had announced that they were five minutes away from Black Eagle. "Quick, Peggy," said Owen, holding her hand and pulling her towards the window. "You must not miss this." As she looked out, all that she could see were clouds. Then, without warning, the clouds disappeared, and they were heading straight for a mountain. The bus wasn't slowing down, and as it came to the rock face it glided right through, as if it wasn't there. Peggy put her hands up over her eyes, and when she put them down, she realised that Black Eagle was inside a mountain.

Chapter 4

THE BLACK EAGLE SCHOOL

The bus stopped and the doors were opened. All the young wizards were scrambling around, picking up their bags and boards, and making for the doors. Fifteen minutes later the bus had disappeared and they were left standing on a long, stone terrace. On one side it looked like the entrance to a castle, and on the other side was a magnificent view of the valley below and the surrounding mountains.

"This way," said Charlie, and guided Peggy towards the castle doors. As the wizards surged forward the mighty doors opened, and they poured through.

"Welcome to the Black Eagle School for Wizards!" boomed a voice. "Please make your way to your houses and report to your teachers. And would Owen Menglor and Peggy Goody please report to Professor Ableman's rooms."

Peggy found it hard to take in. she knew that they were standing inside a mountain, and yet they were out in the open, with a clear blue sky above, and in front of them were green fields that stretched out into the distance. The building stretched down from the front terrace on each side, and was built of stone. It had large, leaded glass windows, and at the end of each building was a stone walkway that led to a central building, with a domed roof.

"I can't believe my eyes," said Peggy, looking at Owen in amazement. "How can all this be possible?"

Owen smiled. "With thousands of years of wizard magic there isn't much our planners can't build. After all, who do you think built the Pyramids and Temples all around the world?"

"The Pyramids! That was the Egyptians," said Peggy.

"Yes, but with wizard planners, not with thousands of slaves and ropes, and hammers and chisels. Without the Levita and Pulshe magic they would never have been built. When you have wizard history lessons you'll find out all about it. But right now we have to go and see Professor Ableman."

They started walking over to the right-hand side of the castle. Owen explained that this side of the castle was where the houses of Goldberg and Redgrave were, and Lister and Bloomsbury where on the other side of the castle. "You probably noticed the big square building in the centre of the walkways; that's where we're going now. It's called the Great Hall. It's where we all go to eat. At the rear of the hall are the headmaster's rooms; they look out over the grounds."

They entered a long, wide corridor, and all the way down, young wizards were saying hello to Owen. He was obviously very popular and well respected. Then at the end of the corridor they turned left, and went through a stone arch that led onto the walkway. This was a stone bridge, and much wider than it first looked from the front of the castle. It was about a fifty-metre walk to the Great Hall.

They crossed and entered the Great Hall. Peggy could see where the name had come from; it was huge. It was laid out symmetrically into four areas, each one in the corner of a central cross walkway. It had neatly spaced-out long wooden tables and wooden benches, and over each quarter hung the house flag. Facing the tables was a platform where the teachers sat and ate.

Owen led the way to a large oak door behind the platform, and knocked.

"Please come in, Owen," said a voice from inside the room. Owen pushed open the door and let Peggy through, and followed her in.

"Ah! Welcome to Black Eagle." The professor's voice was gentle and soothing, and made Peggy feel relaxed. "Please take a seat, and make yourselves comfortable." Professor Ableman was exactly as she had imagined him to be; he was tall and slim, his long hair and beard were silver, and he was wearing full wizard robes. "Peggy, I wanted to have a word with you before you settled in. I have been told much about you, and of your unusual powers. You have a very heavy schedule in front of you, and it is important for you to complete it by the end of the school year. however, having said that, I do not mean that you cannot have fun and enjoy yourself as well.

"I have been informed of the alliance with Owen, Lilly, Charlie, and yourself, and I will endeavour to keep you all together as much as possible; although you should be safe at Black Eagle. But I must stress that you take nothing for granted, and be on your guard at all times. and whatever happens between the four of you, must remain with you.

"In a few days' time, Peggy, I will give you your first wizard history lesson, and tell you how and why we came to live on Earth. Now I would like you both to go and unpack, and get settled in. Am I correct in thinking that you are both in Redgrave?"

"Yes we are, Headmaster," said Owen as he stood up.

"Then I will see you both this evening at the welcoming banquet."

Chapter 5

A CLOSE CALL

P eggy and Owen left the Great Hall and started back across the walkway. They were three metres away from the archway when suddenly there was a rumbling noise from up above. Owen looked up and pushed Peggy so hard she stumbled violently to one side, and he leapt to the other. A split-second later, the top section of a stone chimney smashed onto the ground where they had been standing. It made such a noise that within minutes, the walkway was crowded with wizards all wanting to know what had happened.

"Stand aside!" roared a deep voice. the chattering stopped immediately. It was Professor Battell Crie. Two metres tall, he towered over them all menacingly. He had large, black eyes that looked as if they could pierce through stone, and his large Roman nose snorted like a horse. under his wide lips was a square and powerful jaw. His long, black hair fell across his wide shoulders, and as the crowd parted, he walked towards Owen.

"What has happened here?" he demanded.

Owen looked up at him. "An accident, Professor Crie; one of the old chimneys has crumbled and fell down, but fortunately no one has been hurt."

The professor snorted. "Yes, just as well, just as well. All right, back to your rooms, all of you. Come on, double quick. Not you,

Menglor; stay here," he said, as the crowd disappeared through the door. He turned to Peggy. "You are Peggy Goody, I presume?"

"Yes, I am," she replied.

"Now let me make this clear; this was not an accident. Wizard buildings never just fall down on their own. This was a deliberate attempt to harm you. I promise that I will try to get to the bottom of this. in the meantime, go and get settled in, and I will talk to you at a later date."

Peggy walked into the girls' room. "What took you so long?" Kate enquired. "Come on; you're over here, in between Lilly and me. And this is yours." She pointed to a double-door steel locker. Peggy put her case down on the bed and sat down beside it.

Lilly could sense that something bad had happened. "What's wrong?" she asked.

Peggy shrugged her shoulders and said, "Someone has just tried to kill Owen and me out on the walkway."

"What!?" shouted Kate, her eyes wide open in disbelief.

"How?" Lilly asked.

Peggy explained what had happened with the chimney, and how Owen had pushed her out of the way just in time before it smashed onto the ground where they had both been standing. They all sat down in silence and looked at each other.

In the boys' room, Owen was having the same conversation with Charlie.

"I don't like the sound of this," said Charlie. "We're all supposed to be safe from the outside world while we're inside Black Eagle."

"That's exactly what I was thinking," said Owen. "It's got to be a wizard; but who?"

It was time for everyone to make their way to the Great Hall for the welcoming banquet. "Come on," said Charlie, tugging Owens sleeve. "Let's make sure we get a place for Peggy next to us."

When they got there, the girls had already beaten them to it. "Why are you guys always late? Kate said, laughing at them.

"We do it on purpose so you worry about us," said Charlie.

Kate rolled her eyes and said, "Yeah, Big Deal."

When everyone was seated in their house areas, the hall went quiet, and Professor Ableman stood up. "Welcome back to Black Eagle," he said, holding out his arms. "I hope that, like the professors and I, you are all looking forward to another good year. And just like any other year, we will be saying good-bye to many of our friends and our champions. They will leave us to go out into the world and follow their own paths through life. So please, make sure that you gain as much knowledge from them as you can. Remember; you will be the next champions. Now make your wishes, and let us enjoy the feast.

Peggy looked at Owen with a puzzled expression on her face. "There isn't any food," she said.

Owen smiled. "There is everything that you could possibly desire; but first you have to wish for it. Professor Ableman has cast a spell over all the tables."

Peggy closed her eyes. *Cod, mashed potatoes, peas and parsley sauce.* In a second it was there in front of her on her plate, piping hot.

"What's that?" Charlie asked, looking at her meal and sniffing the air. "It smells like fish."

"It is," she said. "It's cod, and it's my favourite meal ever."

"Cod! Never heard of it," said Charlie. "well, it's not for me," and turned around and bit into a turkey leg, while eyeing up his next plate that had a large helping of chocolate pudding and ice cream on it, just waiting to be devoured.

After they had all eaten their fill, everything on the tables suddenly disappeared and the room fell silent. Professor Ableman stood up. "I would like to welcome all of the first-year students to Black Eagle. There will be a three-day period for you to settle in to your respective houses, and time to meet your teachers, who will in turn show you around the school and some of its surrounding grounds.

"All existing students will have tomorrow to settle in, and then down to work as normal. The house swimming teams will register with Professor Pike, who in turn will issue you with the current year's swimming fixtures. The house surf board polo teams will register with Professor Drakell, who likewise will issue you with the current year's fixtures. The Black Eagle School teams will be picked at a later date. Let me take this opportunity to wish all students a successful year in all that you do. and now please take your time to settle in. Oh! And would Peggy Goody and Owen Menglor please stay behind for a moment?" Peggy and Owen sat down again and waited for the Great Hall to clear.

Professor Ableman called over to them: "Please come to my rooms," and led the way. When they reached the professor's rooms, the door opened. "Please come in and take a seat." As they sat down, the door closed quietly behind them. "I have been informed of the incident earlier, and obviously I am concerned. but what concerns me even more is the lack of danger lessons Peggy has received. I was led to believe that Peggy had been schooled in attack and defence strategy, albeit in a limited way, and yet she has no sense of danger; a crucial lesson, I would have thought."

Owen spoke up. "The fault is mine. I know that it is no excuse, but Peggy has learned her lessons so quickly and so well that I have overlooked the most basic of lessons."

"I have not asked you here to lay blame, and I do realise why it was so easily overlooked. It is a sense that is learned at a very early age, long before you come to school. Nevertheless, in Peggy's position, it is imperative that she learns. Now, Owen, tell Peggy how you knew that the chimney was falling towards you; after all, you were not looking up."

Owen said, "I tasted it. Danger has a taste; everyone knows that." He stopped and realised what he had just said. "That is, everyone except Peggy." He felt really stupid.

The professor looked at the two young wizards and said, "We must all remember that Peggy was one hundred percent human until she was fifteen years old, apart from her fairy magic. Wizards have learned most of the things that they will ever learn by then. We therefore have to be careful that we do not overlook the very basics. Tomorrow may I suggest that you tour the grounds, etcetera, and familiarize yourself with the school?"

"That has all been arranged, Headmaster," said Owen with a snigger on his face. "Angus Fume has already made it a date with Peggy."

"Quite so," said Professor Ableman, and put his hand to his mouth and gave a gentle cough.

On the way back to the dorms, Owen said, "We are meeting up in the Redgrave den in an hour so I'll see you later; try and relax. I think that you and Angus will have a busy day tomorrow."

When Peggy got back, the girls all wanted to know what Professor Ableman had wanted to see her for. Peggy held her hands out and puffed her cheeks. "Apparently I can't taste danger, and I didn't even know it had a taste."

"That's ridiculous," said Kate. "We learn how to taste danger as soon as we can walk; what's so different with you?"

"I've only been a wizard for a few months," said Peggy, "and it's something that I have never been taught to do."

Kate wouldn't let it go. "That's impossible! You are born a wizard; it's not something that happens to you overnight."

"It's true," said Peggy. "Enzebadier the Elder gave permission for me to mix my blood with a wizard and I became a wizard, just a few months ago."

Kate was defiant. "Okay, wizard, I'm going to send you a sting. Let's see what you can do." Peggy faced up to Kate, four metres apart. Her mood changed, and she went into total concentration. Kate drew her wand and sent a sting. Peggy drew her wand with so much speed that no one saw it. Her mind had taken over and sent a Flecta spell at Kate. She jumped back, a look of amazement on her face. "Ouch! How did you do that? You didn't have time!"

Lilly spoke first. "There are lots of things that you will have to accept about Peggy; things that she cannot talk about. But one thing I will tell you is that she also possesses fairy magic, and has the fastest wand that I have ever seen."

Kate sat down on her bed with a thump, and a look of bewilderment on her face. "What else can you do?" she asked. Peggy took Lilly's hand and Hazed; they both disappeared. Kate's mouth dropped open, and then they were back. "Okay," said Kate. "No more questions. I can't take any more; I'm going to bed. See y'all in the morning."

"Wait," said Peggy. "We're supposed to be meeting up with the boys in the den in an hour so that Owen can explain to you all how I have become a wizard, and tell you of my powers."

Kate stood back up. This is something that I have got to hear," she said, and they all nodded.

Chapter 6
THE DEN

Owen waited for them all to sit down and get comfortable; the den was a circular room with a very high ceiling, and seats of various shapes and sizes scattered around it. "OK," said Owen. "Before I start, I want you all to promise me that the story I am about to tell you will go no further than us."

"I promise," they all said together.

"Many years ago, my father was collecting herbs and fungi in the forest near our home, when he came upon a fairy that had become ensnared in a bird trap set by a poacher. She called out to him for help, and my father released her. For his help, an intelligence fairy called Bluebell said that if he ever needed help in any way, he was to call out her name, and she would come and help.

"Many years later, Bluebell herself was involved in an accident in the same forest, but this time much more serious. She was lying badly injured in the top of a tall tree, with her energy and magic slowly ebbing away. In the trees surrounding her were creatures called Demodoms, waiting for her to pass out so that they could capture her and take her back to their master, Demodus.

"This is where Peggy's journey began. She rescued Bluebell, and carried her back to the fairy camp were the Silver Fairy lives in the Silver Cave. Peggy was given fairy magic by the Silver Fairy as a reward for helping Bluebell. She was twelve years old then, and over the next three years she used her magic to save many lives, for which the Golden fairy queen gave her even more magic.

"Demodus is a giant gnome with supernatural tunnelling skills. This has enabled him to tunnel under human homes and rob them, amassing for himself a huge fortune. It was on one of his underground trips that he came up under our home, and it didn't take him long to realise that he had discovered a wizard's home. He returned home and put together a plan to capture my father by gassing him, and taking him back to his underground kingdom.

"My father escaped quite easily, but he had to leave his wand behind because Demodus had hidden it. My father decided to ask for the fairies' help, and so he called out to Bluebell, who came as promised. There was a problem, however; fairies, by their own laws, are not allowed to enter anyone's home without being invited. But they could if someone let them in.

"They called on Peggy, and asked if she would be prepared to help get my father's wand back. It was explained to her how dangerous it would be, and how they would completely understand if she refused. She said yes without a second thought, and then she trained with the fairy army for a week, were she learned to Haze. Then, when she was ready, she went in with Bluebell to retrieve my father's wand. They not only came out with the wand, but found out that Demodus was in possession of the Sword of Destiny."

Charlie jumped to his feet and shouted, "WOW! Isn't that the sword that started the great wizard war with Baldric Zealotte?"

"The very same," said Owen. "And Peggy found it. The Elders gave my father their permission to make Peggy a wizard by mixing his blood with Peggy's in a special ceremony. And here she is: Peggy Goody, wizard with fairy magic and fairy speed."

Kate stood up. "So *that's* how you did it."

"Did what?" asked Owen.

"She sent a sting back to me so fast I didn't even see it."

Charlie spoke up. "Listen, Peggy has total recall, and super speed in everything. And she can make herself invisible, too."

"Tell me, are there any more powers that we should know about?" Kate asked, puffing out her cheeks.

Peggy stood up and moved into the middle of the den and said, "Angus, Charlie, come over here please, and stand by my side." They both got up and went over to Peggy and stood on opposite sides. Put an arm across my shoulders, and lift up the other. She put her arms around their waists and gripped them tightly. "UP-UP," she said, and they all shot up to the ceiling. "Down-Down," and they came back down. And then she went into Haze and they all disappeared.

When she came out of the Haze, they were all in shock; the atmosphere was electric. They all erupted at the same time; Who-How-Where-Why-When, the questions came at Peggy like a machine gun.

Kate was shaking her head. "You can do all of that, but you can't even taste danger? It's unbelievable. And you've only been a wizard for a few months? I don't know about the rest of you, but I need to lie down in a dark room." That made them all burst out into fits of laughter.

"Come on," said Owen. "Let's all go and get a good night's sleep."

Next day they were up early, showered and dressed, and on their way to the Great Hall for breakfast. The whole school was buzzing with excitement. The boys were already there; Charlie's voice could be heard over the others. "Peggy! Over here!" they had got the table organised. Once the table places had been chosen, they kept the same place all year; that is, unless they wanted to exchange with someone. Owen was on the end opposite Lilly, then Charlie and Peggy, Singh and Fatima, and the rest were scattered along the table.

When they were all seated, Professor Ableman stood up and the hall fell silent. "Today is your first full day at Black Eagle, and your first breakfast together. There are two things to remember: one, the seat that you have now will be the seat that you use for the rest of the year. And two, food will be available at the times given on the notice board and will be strictly adhered to. If you are late, you do not eat. So remember to be punctual. Now, enjoy your breakfast. Thank you."

The tables filled with food of all kinds, and everyone started to tuck into it.

Peggy was really feeling at home, and Charlie was teasing her and making her laugh. Suddenly there was a hand on her shoulder. She looked up, and it was Angus. "Have you remembered that I am showing you around the school today, Peggy?" he asked with a big grin on his face.

"Yes, I've remembered," said Peggy. "And I'm really looking forward to it."

"Don't leave me this way, Peggy," mocked Charlie, and pretended to cry into his hands. But deep down, he did feel a little bit jealous. He would have loved to have spent the day with Peggy. But fair dues, Angus had jumped in first and asked her. He had even beat Sal Mendez to the punch, and that took a bit of doing.

Angus was beaming. "I'll meet you after breakfast on the terrace by the main gate, and we can start at the front and work our way around."

"Okay," said Peggy.

"Would you like to borrow a compass?" Charlie offered, grinning from ear to ear.

"Hey, man, get lost, will ya?" said Angus, and walked back to his seat.

Chapter 7
THE TOUR

Aftter breakfast the tables cleared, and Peggy and the girls went back to their room. Peggy decided to change into her trainers to do the tour of the grounds, and was just about to leave to meet Angus when Lilly called to her, "don't forget your board!"

"My board? What for?"

"I don't think you realise how big this place is. When you leave the school, the grounds go on for miles and miles. Trust me, you will need your board."

"Thank you," said Peggy, and gathered up her board, then disappeared through the door.

Angus was waiting for her when she arrived. "I see you brought your board, Peggy. Thank goodness; I forgot to ask you to bring the wee thing along with you."

"Lilly told me that I'd need it to view the grounds."

"So you will, Peggy," said Angus.

"Let's start outside on the balcony and I'll show you the valley." They walked through the massive doors and onto the balcony, and looked down into the most beautiful valley down below.

"It's beautiful," said Peggy and squeezed Angus' hand.

"We're in Wales," he said. "It doesn't get much better than this; except for Scotland, that is," he added, and they both burst out laughing. Little did Peggy know that she was standing in exactly the same spot that Savajic had stood all those years ago when he had first laid eyes on Owen's mother.

They stood for a while, taking in the wonderful view, then turned away and walked back through the doors into the school. thirty metres in was a balustrade that overlooked a large, square grass field about four times the size of a football pitch, and beyond that was the Great Hall. On each side were the school houses. "This is the polo field, where the different houses do battle for the school cup. And when I say *battle*, I mean no quarter is given."

"You've seen our side of the school, so we'll start from the other side. It's very much the same as our side, but you need to know where the other houses are." They walked down the passageway, which was geometrically opposite to theirs, and when they came to the end they turned right and through the arch onto the walkway that led to the Great Hall. There they stopped.

"Right, Peggy, this is where we need our boards." they laid them on the ground and stepped on. "Are you ready?"

"Yes," said Peggy, and they rose into the air, and off they went. After about ten minutes they came up to a large circular building a hundred metres in diameter. It was very strange, with tall, arched windows running all around, equally spaced; but there was no door. They were some twenty metres from the ground, then plain wall for another twenty metres up, and on the top was a shiny copper dome that covered the entire building.

"This is the forbidden library, and the stargazing observatory. We are not allowed to enter unless we have special permission and are accompanied by Professor Gellit."

Peggy gave Angus a puzzled look. "There's no door to the observatory. How would you get in?" As soon as she had finished speaking, a grinding sound started, and the top half of the building began to turn. It stopped, and an arched door appeared in the wall. The door swung open, and at the same time a platform came out from underneath the door. It stopped five metres out.

"Good morning!" said a voice from beyond the door, and out stepped a wizard dressed in a robe and pointed hat that was covered in stars and moons. "I'm Professor Gellit," he said. "Are you interested in our universe?"

"To be honest," said Peggy, "apart from the sun and the moon, I don't know too much about it. But I would really like to learn."

"That's the spirit!" said the professor. "I don't recall seeing you here before. What's your name?"

"Peggy Goody," she said. "It's my first full day here, and Angus has been kind enough to show me around."

"A gentleman indeed," said the professor. "I must remember your name, Peggy, and later you can come and visit me. Now I must go," he said. "I have very important matters to attend to." he turned and went back through the door. The platform slid back in, and the door closed and vanished.

"Are there any more surprises like that?" asked Peggy, puffing out her cheeks.

Angus laughed out loud. "You will have to wait and see. Come on." They glided over a grass plain that went on and on until a vast lake appeared in front of them. "We'll stop here," said Angus, and they gently dropped down to the ground. "This is called Lake Scary, because of the blocker fish and the nibblers. If you look over there you can see an island in the centre of the lake. That's Dragon Island, and that's where the prickly dragon lizards live."

"Each year, a team of final-year wizards from White Eagle race against us across the lake. We have to swim to the island and try to avoid the blocker fish that bump into us as hard as they can; if they stop us, the nibblers start biting. It's very dangerous, and only the very best swimmers take part. Then there's the run across Dragon Island trying to dodge the dragon lizards. They are covered in venomous quills; they won't kill you, but do have a nasty sting. And then it's back into the lake to swim to the other side; but this time it's more dangerous because by now, tiredness is setting in."

"That sounds like some challenge," said Peggy. "Can we fly over and see the dragons?"

"Why not," replied Angus. "But stay in the air." They lifted off and started across the lake. When they got to the island, Peggy looked down and could see the dragon lizards. They were small dragons in every detail except for the tail; halfway down were long, sharp quills, and they had wings, but they were too small to allow them to fly. Peggy thought that they were beautiful, in a rugged sort of way.

"OK," said Angus. "Next stop's the redwood forest." they flew over the lake and over another grass plain, and then they saw it. A massive redwood forest. Peggy had never seen trees so tall.

"They're unbelievable!" said Peggy.

"They are very old," said Angus. "And if you look over there, that one is Pylonius. He is the king of the redwoods. Let's go over and say hello." Pylonius was a massive redwood, at least twenty-five metres in diameter.

"Pylonius, can you hear me?" shouted Angus.

"I can hear you," said a rich, booming voice, and a massive face appeared on the trunk of the tree. "Why have you awoken me? You know that trees sleep in the day."

Angus felt embarrassed. "I'm so sorry," he said, "but I'm showing Peggy around the school and the grounds. She's new, and I wanted her to meet you."

"Quite so, quite so. I'm, Pylonius, king of the redwoods, and it's very nice to meet you, Peggy."

Peggy curtseyed and said, "It's an honour to meet you, King Pylonius."

"Will you be taking part in the Hawk Hunt Championships this year, Peggy?"

"I don't know what they are," said Peggy.

"Never mind, I'm sure Angus will tell you all about it. Now I must get my sleep." The face disappeared.

"Come on," said Angus, and they quietly glided away. "Land here," he said, and they landed on the top of small a hill. "I've brought some sandwiches and lemonade; I hope they're okay."

"Oh, that's great," said Peggy. "How thoughtful of you."

Peggy finished her sandwich and sipped her lemonade. "Angus, what was Pylonius talking about when he mentioned the Hawk Hunt Championships?"

Angus cleared his throat. "Well, when we get to the zoo, I'll show you the Lightning Hawk. It's pure white in colour, with a black lightning streak on each wing. it can fly quicker than any other bird, and its ability to change direction is almost supernatural.

"For the championships, the starting line is a thousand metres inside the forest. We set ourselves on our boards, and on a given signal, the Lightening Hawk is released. It flies to the edge of the forest, and it can take any path between the trees that it chooses. The challenge is to follow in its tracks for as long as you can; but once you get more than twenty metres behind, your run is ended. There are marshals every twenty-five metres who check your distance. As soon as the gap is greater than twenty metres your run is finished, and the distance is measured and recorded against your name.

"The two best surfers from each house are picked and the longest ride wins. If you catch the Lightening Hawk, it's added points for your house. but no one has ever even come close. I said the best surfers and not the fastest, because skill in amongst the trees is probably more important than speed. It's very dangerous, and there have been plenty of broken bones."

"It sounds like fun," said Peggy, casting her mind back to the lessons she'd had in Savajic's forest.

"The championships are held four times a year, and the top six students compete against White Eagle for the fastest wizard cup, which they hold, at the moment.

"Last year, Will Steele from White Eagle came first, pushing the favourite Charlie Manders into second place by the smallest of margins. It caused quite a lot of controversy because Jed and Guy Belbur from White Eagle were marshals, and there was talk of them cheating and fixing the result. Anyway, Peggy, what's your surfing like? Are you any good?"

Peggy felt a bit self-conscious and embarrassed. How could she tell Angus that she was better than Charlie? "I'm okay," she said. "Charlie and Lilly have been helping me."

"Well, you couldn't get better teachers," said Angus. "They really helped me to get into the house polo team.

"Right; if we're finished here, we can get going." he drew his wand and pointed it at the leftovers and said, "Dispro." they vanished immediately.

"Where to next?" asked Peggy, wanting to see more and more of this incredible world called Black Eagle.

Angus' manner suddenly changed. He looked deadly serious and said, "try to imagine that this was an underground world that existed well before it was discovered by the wizards. But in their wisdom, they decided that with some modification it would make a perfect location to build a place of learning, hidden from view from the outside world.

And because of the granite rock that surrounds us it was named Black Eagle. White Eagle was given its name because it lies deep inside chalk cliffs in a place humans call Dover.

"Now, to answer your question, our next journey is across the edge of the Death Swamp. No one knows how old it is, and even less is known of the creatures that inhabit it. all we do know is that to land there is sure death. Many lives have been lost by those who have tried to unlock its secrets. When we start to surf across the swamp we stop for nothing; no matter what you see or hear, you must keep moving, Peggy. Do you understand?"

"Yes," she said, looking a little apprehensive.

"Because it is so dangerous, we will only be crossing the front edge, just to give you an idea of how bad it is." They rose fifty metres into the air and began to move forward. "Stay close," Angus whispered as they increased their speed.

It was a horrible place. Peggy could see the ground moving as worm-like creatures burrowed their way through the mud and water. Trees were moving about on wicked-looking roots. In the distance she could see what looked like a large whirlpool in the sky; it was evil-looking, dark in the centre, with grey and purple rings fanning out, and it was spinning slowly.

Angus pointed to it and said, "That's the worm hole; anything that passes too close will get sucked in, never to be seen again. It is thought that it goes right down to the magma." They were now moving faster than ever. "Keep up!" shouted Angus, and thirty minutes later they had left the Death Swamp behind. "I'm not sure that I did the right thing showing you the Death Swamp, although it was only the very front of it. I hope it didn't scare you too much, Peggy." He had gone deathly pale and had a worried look on his face.

"I'm good," she replied, "but you look really scared; what's happened?"

"Nothing to be bothered about," he said. "I just thought that I'd seen something, that's all. I really do want you to see as much as you can." They had dropped down closer to the ground, and the terrain had changed to a rocky surface. Suddenly they were over a massive, cave-like hole. The walls were sheer, and disappeared into darkness. "This is where the rock face surfing championship trials take place twice a year. We can only practice here under the strict supervision of

Professor Battell Crie. And now, for our last visit of the day, you will like this, Peggy; it's the zoo, and the aviary."

They travelled for a good thirty minutes over what seemed to be an endless grass plain. Then Angus suddenly pointed towards a very unusual-looking building. "There it is!" he shouted. "Over there!" She saw a massive glass dome supported by a circular glass wall some thirty metres high, which itself was encircled by a ring of very large cages.

As they flew in closer, Peggy could see that all of the cages held very strange-looking creatures, and she could hardly wait to see them up close. "Welcome to the zoo and aviary," said Angus. "Where would you like to start?"

"Can we see the birds first?" she asked. she was really excited.

They picked up their boards and walked down a pathway in between two of the cages. Peggy could hear the loud roars of the creatures, but couldn't see any of them. The path led them to a glass door with a notice saying PLEASE RING THE BELL AND WAIT. The bell looked like a rabbit that was disappearing into a hole in a tree. Peggy held the rabbit's tail firmly in her hand and moved it from side to side, and a bell rang out. Through the door they could see a scruffy figure scurrying towards them.

"All right, all right, I can hear you!" shouted a squeaky voice. The door swung open and a small, plump wizard covered in dust and feathers looked up at them and said, "What can I do for you?"

"Hello Professor Gull," said Angus. "I'm sorry to disturb you, but would it be possible for me to show Peggy around your aviary?"

"Well, yes, you can, but I'm afraid that I can't accompany you. I have a batch of five Short Horn Greshlicks hatching, and I can't afford to lose any of them; there are only ten of them in existence."

They walked through the door and closed it carefully after them. "Wow!" said Peggy, catching her breath. "It's amazing!" She knew that she was inside a glass building, but there were no walls or roof; a world of its own, with no barriers; or so it seemed.

Angus was laughing at the expression on Peggy's face. "I told you that you would like it, didn't I? Let's mount our boards," he said. "You could spend a week surfing around here." As they travelled along, Angus was pointing out various species to her; she had never heard of most of them, let alone seen them. Angus suddenly said, "stop!"

Perched on a tree in front of them was a pure-white bird. "That's a Lightening Hawk," whispered Angus. "You know, the bird in the Hawk Hunt Championships."

Angus looked down at his wristwatch. "It's getting late, Peggy. We need to start thinking about getting back."

"OK!" she said, and they turned and headed back to the door. It appeared out of nowhere and opened itself. They went through, and made sure that it was closed behind them.

Peggy asked Angus if the cages were like the aviary. "Good question," said Angus. "As a matter of fact, they are. Once you enter a cage you can travel in any direction for days without seeing a fence of any kind, and each cage has its own climate to suit the creatures that live there. For instance, the White Siberian Fire-breathing Snow Dragon has an ice plain with snow-capped mountains inside. While the three-headed Giant Mongoose has a forest with tropical fruits and nuts to eat.

Peggy said, "Perhaps we could visit just the zoo next time."

"You can bet on that," said Angus, with a grin on his face.

"Come on then, Angus," said Peggy. "Let's get back. Today has been fabulous. Thank you for giving me so much of your time." She leaned forward and kissed him on the cheek.

"The pleasure has all been mine," he said a little awkwardly. They took off and sped towards Black Eagle.

Chapter 8
THE REPORT

They landed back on the walkway next to Redgrave. "You go ahead, Peggy," Angus said. "I just need to see Professor Ableman about something."

"OK," Peggy said, and disappeared.

Angus strode across the walkway at speed and entered the Great Hall. He headed for the headmaster's rooms. he stopped and knocked on the door. "Come in," said a gentle voice, and the door swung open. "Please sit down, Angus, and tell me the reason for your visit."

Angus went over the route that he had taken Peggy on during the day until he came to the Death Swamp. "I saw a wizard enter the Death Swamp and disappear into the worm hole, Professor. I am absolutely certain of it."

Professor Ableman let out a loud sigh and looked concerned. "This confirms my greatest fears, I'm afraid. Professor Gellit and I have been monitoring the swamp for some time now, and yours is the third sighting of a wizard entering the swamp. Three sightings are good enough for me to believe that our security at Black Eagle has been compromised, and our enemy has gained access to us from beyond the Death Swamp. The attempt on the lives of Owen and Peggy is starting to make sense, and we now know that the would-be killer is a wizard.

"Thank you for coming to see me right away, Angus. I would like you to keep this information to yourself, if you would. I don't want the enemy to have any idea that we are on to them."

"Of course," said Angus. "My lips are sealed, Headmaster."

Professor Ableman waited for Angus to leave, then spun around in his chair and pointed his wand at the wall. "Screen!" he commanded, and the wall turned into a giant screen. "Wizard Council!"

The figure of a wizard came into view and said, "Can I help you, Professor Ableman?"

"I need to speak to Enzebadier the Elder on a matter of great importance."

The wizard disappeared from the screen, and Enzebadier appeared almost immediately. "Greetings, Professor Ableman. What a pleasant surprise. I hope it's nothing too serious."

"Yesterday an attempt was made on Peggy Goody's life. We are certain that it was another wizard. This means that the security at Black Eagle has been compromised, and our students are in serious danger. We have had the Death Swamp under surveillance for some time, and today we have had the third sighting of a wizard entering the worm hole."

Enzebadier interrupted, "but we know that the worm hole leads directly to the magma; there would be no return for them. It would be certain death."

"That is what we have always believed," said the professor. "But in what other way could the security have been breached?"

Enzebadier stroked his beard. "Keep the security measures as they are for the time being. I am going to contact Savajic Menglor and ask him to come and see you immediately. Give him all the information you can, and let us see what he can come up with." The screen faded, and the professor sat down behind his desk to ponder the situation.

Chapter 9

SAVAJIC ARRIVES

Fifteen minutes later there was a knock on his door. "Come in," said the professor. The door opened, and in walked Savajic Menglor.

"I got here as quickly as I could," he said. "The news is very disturbing indeed. I hope that Peggy has not been hurt."

"Peggy is fine. Luckily for her she was with Owen when the attempt was made, and he managed to save her from injury. What are your thoughts on this, Savajic?" the professor asked.

"Well, for a start I do not believe that there is a way back from the worm hole. If you remember when I was in my last year here, both I and Fergus Whistlebutt carried out a series of tests on the worm hole. We sent numerous objects directly into the throat of the worm hole and tried to get them back, with no success whatsoever. The conclusion that we came to was that there was no way back.

"Before the new term started, Professor, was there anything different to the normal routine?"

"Well, yes, as a matter of fact there was. Two of our teachers had to be replaced at the last moment because of sickness."

"That is very interesting," said Savajic. "And where exactly did they come from?"

"White Eagle offered to loan them to us until our teachers were well enough to come back."

"Did you ask them if they had any spare teachers?"

"Well, no, they just offered."

"And the replacement teachers; do they teach the same lessons as the teachers that are away sick?"

"Well, yes, as a matter of fact they do," said the professor, a look of disbelief spreading across his face. "Surely you are not suggesting that they deliberately made my teachers sick so that they could put their own teachers in to breach our security?"

Savajic smiled. "I am not ruling anything out at this stage. Let us consider for a moment; how difficult would it be to send a dummy of a wizard into the worm hole? from my own experience I can tell you it would be easy. From a distance it would look real enough, and lead you to think that this was where the danger was coming from. A well-thought-out strategy.

"Now I need to know who the teachers are, and then I need to enlist the help of Peggy Goody. Professor, can you arrange a room for my stay?"

"Of course, Savajic, you are welcome to stay in my guest room. It's a little more private. Before we get ready for dinner, Savajic, I must ask you as a matter of some urgency; why have you neglected to teach Peggy how to taste danger?"

"The answer to that is quite simple," Savajic said. "It's because I can't. As you know, Peggy was born human, and therefore has no Calatum Gland. We can't give her one, so I can't teach her. But all is not lost. I have given the problem a lot of thought, and I intend to ask the Golden Fairy Queen if she could give her animal instinct."

"Oh, well done," the Professor said. "That certainly eases my mind."

The evening meal was a noisy affair, with all the students talking at the same time. Savajic had been announced as an honoured guest of Professor Ableman.

Peggy, Owen, Lilly, and Charlie had been invited to Professor Ableman's rooms after dinner, and as soon as they had finished, they went to their rooms to freshen up, and then they met back down in the Great Hall. By then it was deserted.

"Come on," said Owen, and held Peggy's hand. Lilly and Charlie followed close behind. "Let's go and see what the headmaster wants us for."

Chapter 10

THE ENEMY WITHIN

Owen knocked on the door. "Come in," said the professor. The door swung open, and they walked in. Savajic was standing next to the professor's desk, and motioned them to sit down in chairs that had been arranged in a semi-circle opposite the desk.

Professor Ableman gave a small cough and cleared his throat. "You are probably already aware that up to date, three attempts have now been made on Peggy's life. The first one we believe by Demodus, an enemy of Peggy's, before she became a wizard. But much more serious is that we are sure that the last two attempts have been made by wizards." The professor looked at Savajic. "Will you take it from here?"

"Yes, Headmaster." Savajic leaned against the desk and looked directly at the four young wizards. "Because the attempt on Peggy's life was actually *inside* Black Eagle, we now know that our security has been compromised. This can only be made possible by other wizards.

"Now there have been three definite sightings of wizards entering the worm hole; two by Professor Gellit, and one today by Angus Fume."

Owen and Lilly and Charlie all turned and looked at Peggy. Peggy held up her hands and said, "believe me, I didn't know."

"No, she didn't," the headmaster said. "I swore Angus to secrecy over the matter."

Savajic continued, "When I was in my last year here, I carried out extensive experiments with Fergus Whistlebutt, a close friend of mine. We sent countless items directly into the worm hole, and in every case we failed to retrieve even the smallest item. I am convinced that it is a false trail deliberately laid out to put us off course. So far we have established that two of our own teachers fell mysteriously ill just before the start of a new year. White Eagle stepped in with two replacement teachers, even before we had requested any help. This in itself, to say the least, is suspicious. There is another consideration to be made, one that has only just crossed my mind." turning around to the professor he asked, "have you had any recent requests for permits to visit and stay in the creature zoo from outside study groups?"

"Yes, as a matter of fact I have," said the professor. "There is at the moment a group of six living and working in the Arctic Snow Dragon enclosure. They arrived three weeks ago. My goodness, you don't believe that they are infiltrators, do you, Savajic?"

Savajic stood up and started to pace around the room. "Supposing they were? It would be a perfect cover for them. They could slip in and out without drawing attention to themselves.

"We need a plan of action; Peggy, is it possible for you to Haze the four of you for say, fifteen minutes?"

"I can have a go," said Peggy, standing up and holding out her hands. She looked at the others and said, "Come on, let's try." They all stood up and held hands, and Peggy Hazed. Within seconds, they had all disappeared.

"Hold it," said Savajic. Ten minutes passed, and the Haze was holding. Then fifteen. "Come back," said Savajic, and Peggy came out of Haze. "Well done," said Savajic. "How do you feel, Peggy?"

"Fine," she said. "I didn't use up as much energy as I thought I would."

"This gives us a tremendous advantage," said Savajic. "Now, how do we use it? I believe that we should devote our time and energy to the group in the zoo. I know that the two teachers are suspicious, but they seem a little bit too obvious to me. I think that there are two false trails and one real one; and the two false trails are designed to draw our attention away from the zoo, and waste our time chasing shadows.

"All of this information is to be kept strictly between us six in here. Walls have ears, so be careful what you say and where you say it. Now, for the time being, go about your lessons as normal. But be ready to spring into action at a minute's notice. In the meantime I will set up a camp close to the entrance of the Arctic Snow Dragon enclosure under a 360-degree Parto spell, and monitor all movements."

Chapter 11
LOCKSTAY PRISON

Keymol Locke ran his prison with regimental precision. It was spotlessly clean, and 100 percent secure. There was a place for everything, and everything was in its place. It was visiting day, and the visitors were filing past the two guards at the entrance who were checking their passes. Helen Belbur was standing patiently in line, waiting to see her husband, Sealin Belbur. Sealin was a vicious killer in prison for life for killing an entire family of wizards who were brave enough to stand up against him. She was ushered inside by a guard, and asked to sit in a booth with a screen in front of her that prevented her from passing anything to her husband. A buzzer sounded and a door swung open, and Sealin Belbur came in and sat down, facing her.

"How are you, Sealin?"

"I'm good. What news have you got for me?"

"Your plan for distraction at Black Eagle has been set into motion, and I have been informed that they have fallen for it. Savajic Menglor is already there and investigating."

"Excellent!" said Sealin. We must give them plenty to think about. I want you to make sure that they keep me informed about every move they make. And by the way, did we manage to get rid of Peggy Goody?"

"No," said Helen. "I think that she could be quite a nuisance to us; anyway, I have given out instructions to kill her at the first opportunity that we get."

Sealin Belbur was grinning from ear to ear. "So far, so good," he said. "We must keep our real secret under wraps at all cost. Now, what news do you bring me about the bridge over the worm fields?"

"The news is all good. We are making wonderful progress. We have two of the best planners working for us; Brixun Mortah and Showvel Hanpix. Their families are under guard, and the Death Riders have orders to kill them all if our bridge-building plans are compromised by them. I have been informed that the bridge will be complete and span the worm fields in seven months. Our planners have perfected a way of building behind and underneath an elaborate façade that blends in perfectly with the worm fields."

"And how are the Hobgoblins? Are their preparations going well?" Sealin asked.

"Almost too good," Helen said with a smile. "They are so ready to do battle with the Gnomes that we might have trouble holding them back once the bridge is complete."

"Well, the answer to that problem is simple," he replied. "We complete the last section when we are ready to go, and not before."

Helen looked puzzled, and asked Sealin why the Hobgoblins are so terrified of the worm fields. Sealin crossed his arms. "It's a strange story," he said. "Over two thousand years ago, the worm fields were the Gnomes' richest mining area; they mined millions of tons of copper and tin. The mines stretched the whole length of their borders and were ten miles wide. When eventually they ran out of ore, they were all abandoned. Nobody knows where they came from, but the mines became infested with Snackfast worms. Over the centuries, they managed to dig their way up to the surface to let in air and feed on the lush grass. This peppered the land with millions of holes. And over time, the holes were covered over with grass. Anyone or any beast that tried to cross the fields would fall victim to the worms; nothing has ever survived the worms. And so by pure chance, the Gnomes have had a perfect defence barrier between themselves and the Hobgoblins; that is, until now. And I have convinced the Black Watch and Death Riders that when Baldric Zealotte returns, with his help we will rain hell on the Gnome nation and claim it for our own, and then make

Zealotte the king. Then we will turn our attention to the Hobgoblins, destroy the bridge, and drive them back into the worm fields. The worms will do the rest. But until then, secrecy is our most important weapon."

"Do our sons know about this?" Helen asked.

"No, they do not!" snapped Sealin. "And they must not know under any circumstances. Do you understand me?" He glared at Helen. "You know how hot-headed those pair are; it would be general gossip within days."

"I'm sorry, Sealin," mumbled Helen. "I had no intention of telling them." the buzzer went, and Helen was glad it was time to go. She said good-bye and left.

Chapter 12
THE HIDE

S avajic was in his sixth week of observation in the hide, and had built up a comprehensive pattern of the group's movements. Professor Gellit had reported three more sightings of wizards entering the worm hole, and Savajic was beginning to think that the whole pattern of things was looking far too familiar.

Peggy had been concentrating on her lessons and was really enjoying them. She had played her first game of surf polo, and Charlie said that she was a natural at it. Helda Scelda had talked her into joining the swimming team, and to Helda's joy, Peggy was quicker than anyone, including Helda herself. Now she was trying to talk Peggy into taking part in the Scary Lake Swim. Peggy couldn't believe how funny Helda was; she had a wicked sense of humour that had her in fits of laughter, and she loved being in her company.

Owen had at last opened up and told Lilly of his feelings for her, and she had told him that she felt the same. It had all been very romantic, and they had sealed it with a moonlit kiss. They already shared most of the same lessons, and they both surfed and practiced together on the polo field, so it was great to know that they were happy with each other's company.

In the meantime, Sal Mendez had tried to woo Peggy with his charm, much to the distaste of Angus Fume, who was a little bit jealous. But both of them were piped to the post by Charlie Manders, who whisked Peggy off somewhere at every opportunity, and Peggy loved it. Peggy and Charlie were really becoming soul mates; he really looked after her, making sure that everything went smoothly for her.

Savajic decided to call another meeting in Professor Ableman's rooms. He was not happy. Things were not right, and he could feel it. All of the group's movements were too regimented. Everybody did the same identical thing at the same identical time, day in and day out; it wasn't natural. He had reasoned that the whole thing was a setup, but why?

They were all assembled in the headmaster's room and Savajic took the floor. "I have called us all together to give you my conclusions for the last six weeks. Every single day I have been monitoring the movements of the group in the Arctic Snow Dragon enclosure, and every single day it has been identical, to the minute. This behaviour is not natural. This leads me to conclude that we are deliberately being misled for some ulterior motive. There is no doubt that the two teachers and the group have been planted here for a reason, and so was the poor attempt to make us think that the worm hole was a way into Black Eagle. And now when I think of the attempt to harm Peggy, that, too, was also very clumsy; but I have to admit, it certainly got my attention. Peggy, I need your help on this one."

"Sure," said Peggy. "What do you want me to do?"

"I know the exact times when one of the group opens the door and comes out, and how long he is gone before he comes back. If we can be waiting outside, Hazing when he opens the door, we can slip in without being noticed. then we have a given amount of time to locate the rest of the group and listen to what they are saying. There is just a chance that they may let something slip when they are talking to each other."

"When do we start?" asked Peggy.

"Tomorrow morning," Savajic replied. "That is, if it is all right with you, Headmaster."

"Of course," said Professor Ableman. "Of course."

"Then, Peggy, will you meet me here tomorrow after breakfast?"

Peggy said, "Yes I'll be here. Will I need my board?"

"Yes, bring it with you. we will need to get to the hide as quickly as possible and well out of sight, and then we wait. And dress in something warm tomorrow, Peggy, because the temperature is freezing inside the Arctic Snow Dragon enclosure.

"Now, before you go, I must remind you that what you have heard tonight is for our ears only. At this point we cannot trust anyone. Now I will say good night."

The next morning after breakfast, Peggy excused herself by saying that she had a lesson with Professor Ableman. Thankfully no one asked her any questions, to her relief; she hated telling lies, even small ones.

Ten minutes later, she was talking to Savajic in the headmaster's room. He was explaining to her that as soon as they were inside the enclosure they could come out of Haze, and he would put up a façade for them to hide behind. "Have you taken any anti-scent potion?" he asked.

Peggy smiled. "Yes I have," she said. She had learned to make the potion in Savajic's workshop, and he had stressed to her how important it was that she take it before going on any kind of mission.

"It's time to go," said Savajic. "Are you ready, Peggy?"

"Yes," she replied. Her heart was thumping with excitement, and she was determined not to let Savajic down. They mounted their boards and shot high up into the air.

"Follow me," said Savajic, and they disappeared into the distance. As soon as they reached the hide, they sat down and relaxed behind the façade.

Chapter 13
THE PLAN

S avajic began to go over his plan with Peggy. "At 10.15 a.m. we go into Haze and make our way to the enclosure door. Then 10.30 a.m. is when one of the group comes out and flies off for exactly one and a half hours. We have to get in and locate the rest of the group and try to find out what they are doing. I have assumed that this will not be an easy thing to do because they may well have put up defences, expecting us to try something like this.

"Whoever put this plan together is a formidable foe and very clever, but we have two weapons that they do not know of; I have developed an anti-façade ray that no one but you and I know of, and best of all, we can Haze. This means that we can see them, but they can't see us. A pretty powerful combination, don't you think?"

Peggy looked at Savajic. She felt so safe when he was with her, and she admired the way he reasoned everything out to the last detail. *One day*, she thought, *I will be like him*. Then she snapped back into concentration mode. Savajic had given the order to Haze. She picked up her board, held Savajic's hand, and Hazed.

They were jogging across the grass towards the door of the enclosure. Savajic had timed it to perfection. The door opened out wide, and a wizard came flying out on his board. Savajic pulled Peggy close to him and they slipped through the door before it had a chance to close.

"That's the easy part over with," whispered Savajic. "Now, Peggy, we need to mount or boards and keep close, and stay in Haze until I have put the façade in place. I will scan in an arc directly in front of us, and if you see anything unusual, squeeze my hand and we will stop. I will do exactly the same. Are you happy with that?"

"Yes," whispered Peggy, and they moved off. Two minutes later the façade was in place, and Savajic told Peggy to come out of Haze.

They had been travelling for about thirty-five minutes when Savajic said, "Peggy, we are reaching a point of no return. Five more minutes and we must go back." Then they heard it; an ear-splitting roar followed by terrified screaming. Suddenly, in front of them was an enormous Snow Dragon. Somehow it had found the group of wizards and had cornered them in between the large rocks at the base of a mountain. It was breathing flames directly at them and they were burning; the screaming was terrible.

Peggy was on the move before Savajic could stop her, and she flew up high over the dragon at a blistering speed. Then she was looping around and started flying directly at the dragon. Her wand flashed out and pointed at the dragon, and she screamed, "Flecta!" at the top of her voice. The flames shot back and engulfed the dragon. It roared and recoiled, and didn't get a second chance to use its fiery breath. In a flash Peggy pointed her wand at a large rock. "Levita!" The rock shot up into the air. "Pulshe!" Her wand flashed into action and the rock smashed into the dragon's head, almost separating it from its body. The dragon fell to the floor, dead. It was all over. Peggy landed next to the wizards, who were badly burned and were dying. Savajic had come over and was trying to comfort them, but only one of them was still alive. He put out his hand and grabbed Savajic's arm. Savajic put his ear close to the wizard's mouth and he whispered something to him but it was garbled. Then he blinked, his eyes rolled back, and he died.

Peggy sat by the corpses and wept. She wasn't ready for this. why did the world have to be so cruel? She felt Savajic's gentle touch on her shoulder. "We must move on, Peggy. Let's go."

"Who are you?" The voice came from behind them; instinctively both Peggy and Savajic were pointing their wands in the direction of the voice. "Don't kill me!" the voice pleaded, and the wizard that had left the enclosure earlier stepped forward towards them.

"Now would be a very good time to tell us who you are and why you are here, and I will not ask you twice." Savajic's voice was threatening.

"I'm just making up the numbers, please, believe me. I was ordered to come here by a member of the Black Watch; we all were. We were given instructions to stay in the enclosure and make regular trips out into the grounds, all lasting one and a half hours, four times a day, and to keep doing it until we were told to go home."

"And was it you who were sending figures of wizards into the worm hole?"

"Yes," said the wizard. "It was us."

"Who makes contact with you, and when?" Savajic's eyes glared at the wizard and he spat out the question in a venomous hiss.

"I don't know," stammered the wizard. "We have never been contacted, not even once since we first came here."

"Then you will stay here until they do contact you. Is that understood? Believe me, if you try to escape, I will personally kill you."

"I promise you that I will stay, you have my word," said the wizard.

"What about the dead bodies?" Peggy said, gesturing over to the dead wizards.

"I will take care of them," said the wizard. "They were all good friends of mine. I can't believe that this has happened. We were told that it would be safe, just as long as we did exactly what we were told." He fell down on his knees and began to sob.

"We must go, Peggy, now!" Savajic's voice made Peggy jump. she picked up her board and started to follow him towards the door. "There is no need to Haze any further," Savajic said. "This part of the game is well and truly over with now." Once they were outside the enclosure, Savajic sped up and headed back to Black Eagle. As soon as they were back, they headed straight for Professor Ableman's rooms.

Chapter 14

THE REVELATION

They made themselves comfortable, and Savajic began to tell their story. He had been right about the worm hole, and right about the activity in the enclosure. Although he thought that the two new teachers were genuine, he would still have them watched. Professor Ableman was amazed, and very disturbed at how easily the Black Watch had compromised the school's security. "This is a wakeup call," he said. "We have had the same spells in place ever since Baldric Zealotte invaded Black Eagle all those years ago."

"Now, Professor, for the bad news, I'm afraid. When we came across the group of wizards, they were under attack from a Snow Dragon, and unfortunately we were too late to save them. They were very badly burned, and they died before we could give them any help; unfortunately, the dragon is also dead. We had no other choice.

There is, however, one wizard still alive in the enclosure. I have given him instructions to stay there until he is contacted by a member of the Black Watch, and to make no mention that we are on to them."

"Very well," Professor Ableman said. "I will contact Professor Grimlook and inform him of the tragedy, and he can do the rest. As far as he is concerned, all he will be told is that a group of wizards on a fact-finding course have met with a terrible accident, and the remaining wizard managed to kill the dragon. How the dragon actually died is of no interest to me, so as far as I am concerned, the matter is now closed. Was there anything else that you found out that might shed any more light on this undercover plan?"

"Well," Savajic said, "by their own admission, we now know for certain that the Black Watch are in control of this. But what I can't figure out is why. What are they trying to hide?" Savajic suddenly snapped his fingers. "I have just remembered," he said. "I managed to get to one of the group before he died and he mumbled something like 'beware of the worm fields.' I have absolutely no idea what he meant."

"I have," Professor Ableman said, "but what it has to do with any of this affair is a mystery to me. As you know, I have dedicated a large part of my time to studying wizard history. And going back to the Great Wizard War, I do recall that Baldric Zealotte had his base in Hobgoblin territory. Now, part of Zealotte's deal with the Hobgoblin king was that if they helped him gain supreme power in the wizard world, he would in turn help the Hobgoblins to conquer the Gnome kingdom. But as we know, Goodrick the Elder trapped him in a time bubble and sent him spinning into space before he could complete his evil plan.

"The Hobgoblins have wanted to go to war with the Gnomes for centuries, but one thing stood in their way; a fearsome, natural barrier. The dreaded Worm Fields," said the professor.

"Worm Fields?" echoed Savajic. "What are they?"

The Professor stroked his beard. "About two thousand years ago, the Gnomes were probably the most prolific miners of all time. and they had a land that was rich in copper and tin. This gave the Gnome nation vast wealth and turned them into a nation of traders. But it caused great resentment and jealousy with their neighbours, the Hobgoblins, who became their number one enemy. Fortunately for the Gnomes, when eventually the copper and tin ore ran out, it left behind thousands of miles of tunnels that stretched the whole length of the border between themselves and the Hobgoblins.

"No one really knows how, but the mines became infested with Snackfast Worms; these are worms that will eat anything from meat to vegetation. Over the centuries, the worms managed to burrow their way up to the surface and feed on the rich grass above, and in turn this has left behind millions of holes that drop down directly to the mines, and of course, to the worms. Because the grass is so rich it covers the holes, and if you are unfortunate enough to find one it is already too late; you will be on the way down to the worms.

"The Hobgoblins are terrified to go near the worm fields, and so the Gnomes have enjoyed peace for many centuries. Now let us suppose that the Black Watch have brokered a deal with the Hobgoblins in anticipation of Zealotte's return to earth. What could it be?" A silence fell over the room while they pondered the professor's question.

Peggy broke the silence first. "If Zealotte promised to help the Hobgoblins to attack the Gnomes all those years ago, he must have had a plan to get the Hobgoblins over the Worm Fields, so the Black Watch must be planning the same. But how?"

Savajic jumped to his feet. "Of course!" he said. "Well done, Peggy."

Peggy looked at him in surprise. "What did I say?"

"They are going to build a bridge! That's what they are doing, and they obviously want to keep it a secret from us. So they have set up this elaborate ruse to keep us occupied while they can go about their evil plans unhindered. Well, this time it has well and truly backfired."

Chapter 15

THE SEARCH

Savajic was pacing around the professor's room. "I must leave immediately," he said. "I need to talk to Enzebadier the Elder. Professor, will you please contact him and tell him that I am on my way?" Savajic held Peggy's hands. "I'm sorry to leave you like this, but I have got to call a meeting. I will contact you as soon as I can." He nodded to the professor and left.

Peggy sat quietly in the chair; her thoughts were in turmoil. She had witnessed the deaths of the wizards, and she had killed a Snow Dragon, a massive and powerful creature. She had acted out of pure instinct and at alarming speed. *Am I turning into a killer?* She asked herself. It seemed such a fine line between killing and acting in self-defence.

Professor Ableman's soft voice came drifting into her thoughts. "Peggy, you seem troubled. Is there something that you would like to talk to me about?"

Peggy looked into his eyes and said, "Professor, it was me who killed the Snow Dragon."

"I know it was," said the professor. "I could see it in your eyes. But sometimes we are called upon to take action to prevent death and destruction to others. In most cases we do not have the luxury of time in which to analyse the situation and make the perfect decision. A split second can be the difference between life and death.

"In the case of the Snow Dragon, it was actually burning the group of wizards, with the intention of killing them all. It was already too late to throw a Proti spell and protect them, and since you had no way to put out the flames, the best thing was to send the flames back to where they had come from, in this case the Snow Dragon. The next thing was to make sure that the flames would not come back. So you killed the dragon. You have nothing to reproach yourself for, Peggy, nothing at all. And remember, the Snow Dragon's next target could well have been Savajic and yourself."

Peggy was feeling more reassured now. "What will happen now, Professor?"

"Well, Peggy, I think that we must wait and see what happens in the meeting between Savajic and Enzebadier. In the meantime, I suggest that you return to your classes and act as normal as possible, and wait for Savajic to return."

Savajic was already in deep conversation with Enzebadier. "If you are correct in your assumptions, Savajic, do you realise what this means?"

"Yes, it means that some of our most distinguished planners and builders have fallen in league with the Black Watch, or are working under threat of violence towards their families."

"More worrying for me," Enzebadier said, "is the fact that at least two of the chamber members are possibly involved, and maybe more. I can't believe that this has happened without us picking up even the slightest hint. And I must also ask the question, dread the thought; are some of our own intelligence involved? We need to convene the war council immediately, and work on a plan to put an end to this before Baldric Zealotte can gain any kind of advantage from this."

"Before you do, Enzebadier, I would like a chance to check out my suspicions before we inform anyone of my findings. I need to catch them red-handed, and get as much information and as many names as I possibly can. If they are not aware that we are on to them, we may be able to use all their work and effort to our own advantage."

Enzebadier stroked his beard and thought for a while. "Of course, you are right," he said to Savajic. "We do not want to go blundering into something only to find out that we were wrong.

"I will leave you to sort out your own reconnaissance plan, and please report your findings to me as soon as you have something concrete." He looked Savajic in the eyes and said, "Please be careful. You know that the Death Riders will not take prisoners."

Savajic stood up and stretched his arms out in front, then he relaxed and tapped his wand. "I won't either," he said.

Savajic suddenly appeared at home in the Great Hall. He was using his Transference spell more and more, and found it to be much more convenient and quicker than travelling by car. He went directly down to his workshop and began working on a plan.

Chapter 16

WIZARD HISTORY

Peggy knocked on Professor Ableman's door. "Please come in, Peggy," the professor called out to her. She opened the door, walked in, and closed the door behind her. The professor had arranged two chairs opposite each other. "Come and sit down, Peggy," he said, gesturing to one of the chairs, and he sat down in the other.

"I am going to start your lesson at the very beginning of time. About six billion years ago, the world was a molten ball of rock and gas, and about four billion years ago, the surface cooled and hardened.

"Life on Earth is primarily responsible for the chemical makeup of the Earth's crust. As oxygen is a by-product of photosynthesis, large amounts of oxygen have been released over the Earth's history, and more than 99% of the crust is composed of various oxides. I will not go into any more detail, but I need you to know a little of the Earth's beginning.

"The wizard world has no God, like the human world has. We have a creator called Gasieus.

"Gasieus used billions of tons of oxygen to create the Earth's layer as we now know it, and then created the Earth's water from hydrogen and oxygen. We believe that Gasieus is both male and female, and we believe that Gasieus created Mother Earth, who in turn has given life to every living thing on Earth. Gasieus is the air that we breathe and the water that we drink. Without Gasieus there would be no life; Gasieus is the creator, and he is part of every living thing.

"We believe in Kanzil, lord of the magma. He pollutes the world with pestilence, war, and famine; he is all powerful, but is contained within the Earth's crust, and this angers him greatly. He shows his anger with volcanoes and earthquakes. He has the power to destroy the world, but if he did he would destroy himself at the same time, so this keeps him in check.

"Kanzil is the source of all that is evil in the world, and he is the creator of Black Magic. Black Magic is the oldest and most powerful of all magic, but to obtain it, you must first sell your soul to Kanzil.

"Kanzil can take many forms, and is in many bodies, including humans and wizards alike. One thing that you can be sure of is that if you sell your soul to Kanzil you will have great power on Earth, but the cost will also be great; the moment you die, Kanzil will come for your soul, and you will burn in the magma for eternity.

"Wizards came to Earth from a distant planet called Wizmo. Our planet, unlike yours, had a very thin and fragile crust, and we lived in constant threat of Wizmo exploding. And one day it did just that.

"Wizards have always been stargazers, and much of our lives were, and still are, influenced by the stars. Our astronomers had been searching for another planet similar to our own, and after many hundreds of years searching the skies, we found Earth. Our Elders had worked out a way to use magic time bubbles and project them into an orbit that would send them to Earth, and on contact they would open.

"Wizmo eventually exploded, with devastating consequences, and only five hundred wizards survived the perilous journey. We landed on Earth about one hundred and twenty thousand years ago, and were scattered around the world in many countries. We found that for some unknown reason, our magic powers had increased, and that helped us to adapt to life on Earth. The air was oxygen-rich and the water was free of sulphur, and there was an abundance of food. We knew that we had landed on a truly superior word.

"Over the millenniums, we have watched as the mammal species on Earth have evolved, and witnessed the superiority that the humans have gained. As time moved on, we managed to blend in with the human race, helping them with building great cities and monuments. But our magic was drawing too much attention to us, so we withdrew to a fourth dimension. It is still not perfect, and we have to be careful how we go about our lives, but it works pretty well. Humans are aware of wizards, but no one can actually say that they have ever seen or known one."

The professor spent the next hour explaining how through the millenniums they had aided the human race with their building knowledge, and how they had given them simple tools like the plough and the wheel and numbers and letters, and how they had taught them about the stars and how to use them to navigate.

Then he came to the Great Wizard War. "It had devastated the wizard population, and whole bloodlines had been lost for ever. Black Magic had prevailed. Kanzil had taken over Baldric Zealotte; a vile and evil wizard who had been planning to kill the Elders and proclaim himself lord of the wizards. Through Black Magic, Zealotte had found a way to contact Kanzil, and when he did, he made a pact with him; Kanzil had fashioned the Sword of Destiny from the heart of the magma and gave it, with all its powers, to Zealotte, in exchange for his soul when he died.

"Zealotte used the sword and its powers in a devastating way; he formed his group of followers and named them the Death Riders. His slaughter of innocent wizards was relentless, and he took it right up to the gates of the Black Eagle School for Wizards, where he trapped Goodrick the Elder. But his arrogance knew no bounds; it was on the terrace at the entrance to the school that Zealotte had boasted to Goodrick that he did not need the power of the sword to kill him. And as Zealotte turned to lean the sword against the school gate, Goodrick struck, and trapped him in a time bubble. He wasted no time, and sent him spinning off into space. It was hoped that eventually Zealotte would land on some far distant planet and the time bubble would open, leaving him there to spend the rest of his life. We now know differently, and should he land back on Earth, he will still have his wand, and all of his Black Magic power. The first thing that he will do is to try and locate the Sword of Destiny. And if he should get it back, then the consequences for the wizard world will be devastating. With Zealotte gone we were able to quell the rebellion, and the wizard world was saved. On that note," said Professor Ableman, "I think that we have covered quite a lot of ground today. I hoped that you enjoyed it."

"Can I ask you a few questions, Professor?" Peggy said.

"Of course you can. What would you like to ask me?" The professor was pleased that Peggy was so interested.

"Well, when you talk of Kanzil and the magma, is that the Devil and Hell in human terms? And is Gasieus our God? Because we believe that our God is in everyone, too."

"Good questions, Peggy, and of course you are right. We all have different names for our gods and devils; but it all comes back to one Creator, and one Kanzil. Any more questions, Peggy?"

"Just the one, Professor," she replied. "You say that Gasieus is male and female. If so, how do we get men and women?"

"Again, another good question, Peggy. let me try to explain it to you. Gasieus created Mother Nature, and gave her the responsibility of making a world that could populate itself without any ongoing help from her. Gasieus gave her his DNA to work with, and she separated it to make male and female creatures, humans, of course, just being one of the many thousands of species."

"Oh! Just one more question, if I may," Peggy asked. "I know that it is important for us to keep our wands safe at all times, because it is part of our power, but I have never asked why."

"This is something that you should understand, and I am glad that you have asked me. It is a question that a wizard would never think of asking because they are born with certain things that are alien to humans. Let me explain.

"For centuries, human scholars have searched for what they call the old knowledge. They believe that there are old books hidden somewhere that would unlock the secrets of the universe; secrets that have vast powers. The truth is that no such books exist. If you can imagine the most powerful computer that exists in the world today and multiply it by at least a thousand times, then you come close to the power of the human brain. The problem for the human race is that it is not capable of unlocking its power or potential, and the reason for that is because, unlike wizards, they have no Ailizium chemical in their bloodstream to activate the brain cells and unlock the massive power it possesses. Wizards have this chemical in their blood, and by the power of thought, can unlock huge amounts of power; some more than others. But to unleash it, it needs a Portal, and the most-used Portal is your wand. But there can be others, like a surf board used for travel, and so on.

Peggy stood up and said, "thank you for spending so much of your time with me, Professor. It's been a wonderful afternoon."

"The pleasure was mine," replied the professor.

Chapter 17
THE BRIDGE

Savajic was ready to go. He had studied the border land between the Gnome kingdom and the Hobgoblins. It was a stretch of land that lay between two mountain ranges, and was some fifty miles long. It was a lovely looking green sea of grass, but hidden in there were the worm fields. He had no idea of the exact location of the bridge for certain, but he had reasoned that it would lie somewhere in the middle so that an army could cross the bridge and deploy equally to the right and to the left; it was what he would do.

He had set his coordinates to land in the centre of the border land and two miles into Hobgoblin territory. This would keep him a safe distance from the bridge, and hopefully he would not be noticed before he set up a Parto spell. He went down his list a final time to double check himself. He was wearing his Transference pendant; "tic." He had his anti-façade baton; "tic." He had taken his anti-odour drink; "tic." He had his powerful binoculars; "tic." He had his holograph camera strapped to his chest; "tic." And a small pack of provisions on his back. He tucked his surfboard under his arm, held his pendant, and gave the command, "Transfer."

He landed quietly on top of a mound and immediately threw up a façade. Now he could relax, and he sat down. He lifted his binoculars and began scouring his surroundings; he stopped when he came to a wide roadway. There he could see the first signs of wizard activity;

large sheets of blue/grey slate were floating in the air and being guided along by Hobgoblins, the same magic that the wizards had used to transport the massive blocks of stone across the Egyptian desert to build the pyramids thousands of years ago. Savajic smiled. He thought to himself, *nothing really changes; instead of slaves, it's Hobgoblins.*

His plan now was to get down to the road and surf alongside one of the sheets of slate behind a façade. He had to keep in the air so that he didn't leave any tracks. He floated down and took position alongside one of the sheets of slate. He estimated that because of the coordinates he had set, the bridge would be about two miles away. He knew that he had to be patient and not rush away to the bridge; this way he would get to know what the approach to the bridge looked like.

Twenty minutes later, he had his answer. The structure was massive. It was twenty-five yards wide, with walls on each side that were six feet high. The Hobgoblins were so frightened of the worm fields that they had to have walls each side to stop them from falling off the bridge. This was truly a bridge of huge proportions. It was being built for an army to cross in great numbers. The Hobgoblin preparations for war were well and truly under way.

Savajic broke away from the road and began to follow the bridge. He climbed higher so that he could see who was doing what. As he had expected, the planners had thrown up a façade to hide what they were doing. He took his anti-façade baton and turned it on; he could see the frenzied activity going on, and to his amazement, he saw two Trolls. They must be in league with the Hobgoblins, he thought. This was very bad news. The Trolls are fearsome warriors, and have powerful magic that will ward off most of the spells that the wizards could send: the Gnomes would be at their mercy. The two that he was looking at were at least twenty-five feet tall and powerfully built. There were estimated to be about three hundred Trolls still alive today, and if they all stood together with the Hobgoblins, they could prove to be a deciding factor in any battle that took place.

Savajic decided to capture the whole length of the bridge on his hologram camera. He panned slowly along, trying hard not to miss even the slightest detail. And as he went along, he was dismayed to see so many wizards; he knew that he would see some wizards, and some that he knew personally, and others that would probably be members of the Black Watch, there to keep the pressure on the planners. As he panned along he recognised two top wizard planners. He was not really surprised. This was a major project, and needed the best planners to bring it all together.

When he came to the end of the workings, he realised that the bridge was suspended some twenty feet from the ground. There must be a reason for this, he thought, and decided that he had all the evidence he needed safely recorded. He now needed to get back and go through a debriefing with the war council. He flew high in the air and headed back to his camp. He tidied up so that no trace of his visit was left behind, then he removed the façade, held his pendant, and gave the command, "Home."

He appeared back home in the Great Hall, and immediately went down to his workshop and began to spread all his equipment out onto his workbench. He was pleased with his morning's work; it had all gone smoothly. but he was also saddened by what he had seen. Savajic suddenly felt hungry. He decided to take a shower and get changed into something more comfortable and then have some lunch. Later he would go back to Black Eagle and contact Enzebadier the Elder from there.

After Savajic finished lunch, he returned to his workshop. There was something that he had to do before going back to Black Eagle. He stood by his workbench and said out loud, "Blue Flash Help." There was a flash of blue light, and Bluebell was standing in Savajic's workshop.

"Greetings, Savajic," she said, smiling at him.

Savajic held out his hand and greeted Bluebell. "It's so nice to see you again," he said. "I am sorry if I have taken you away from anything important."

"Not at all," said Bluebell. "How can I help you?"

"Well, actually, it's something that you may be able to do for Peggy," said Savajic, and sat down in his chair. "There has been another attempt on Peggy's life, actually in the grounds of Black Eagle."

"I thought that was impossible!" said Bluebell. "Isn't there an Exclusion spell covering the entire school?"

"There is," he said. "But somehow it's been breached."

"But now back to the reason why I called out to you for your help. As you know, Peggy was born human, and therefore she has no

Calatium Gland, like the wizards have. So in turn, we cannot teach her to taste danger. I would like to know if it is possible to give Peggy animal instinct."

"Yes, it is," said Bluebell, "but I would have to ask the Silver Fairy, because it is giving Peggy more fairy magic."

"I can understand that," said Savajic. "It's just that Peggy is so vulnerable to attack, and it worries us greatly."

"I will go back and pose the question to the Silver Fairy," said Bluebell, "and then I will return with the answer."

"Thank you," said Savajic. There was a flash of blue light, and Bluebell was gone.

Savajic picked up his hologram camera and slung it over his shoulder, and then he held his pendant and said, "Black Eagle." In a flash he was back at Black Eagle, and he started heading for Professor Ableman's room.

"Welcome back, Savajic. What news have you brought?"

"I was right," said Savajic. "The Hobgoblins are building a bridge. It's a huge structure, and I counted two of our top planners working there. But before I go into detail, could we contact Enzebadier on the screen, so that we can all discuss our next move?"

The professor turned and faced the wall. "Screen," he commanded, and the whole wall lit up.

A life-size wizard appeared on the screen. "How can I help you, Headmaster?" he enquired.

I need to speak with Enzebadier the Elder immediately. It is of paramount importance." The wizard disappeared, and standing in his place was Enzebadier.

"Savajic, I see that you are back. I trust that you had a successful trip."

"Yes, thank you," said Savajic, and began a detailed report of what he had seen.

Both Enzebadier and Ableman could hardly believe what they were hearing. they both looked to be in a state of shock. Savajic broke the silence. "I believe the next move that we make should be to involve Commander Churmill, and him alone. I think that we should give him the camera, and get him to pick his most trusted team to analyse it in detail. We need to have a list of every wizard's name shown on the hologram, so that we can check on them and their families. We need to know who is under threat. We will need estimations on how far the bridge has progressed and a possible completion date; any scrap of information is important. If I get the camera to you, Enzebadier, will you organise the rest with Commander Churmill?"

"Yes, I will," replied Enzebadier. "Get it to me as soon as you can. And in the meantime, I will contact the commander and bring him up to date." The screen disappeared, and the wall was back.

Chapter 18
BATTELL CRIE

There was a loud knock on Professor Ableman's door. "Come in," said the professor. The door swung open, and the large figure of Professor Battell Crie came bounding in.

He nodded at Savajic. "I'm glad I caught you, Savajic," he said. "Because what I've come to see the headmaster about concerns you, too."

"What's the problem, Battell?" Savajic asked.

"It's Peggy Goody," he replied. "I'm worried about her. I took her for her first lesson in battle strategy. Her speed and her ability to learn are unbelievably good, but she has little or no sense of danger whatsoever. She is easily fooled, and far too trusting."

"May I answer that?" Savajic responded.

"Peggy has only been a wizard for a few months."

Battell cut in, "that's ridiculous. She is far more advanced than any wizard of her age that I have knowledge of.

"Nevertheless, it is true. She became a wizard by mixing blood with me in a ceremony condoned by the Elders just a few months ago. But up until then she was human, and because of that she was born without a Calatium Gland, and therefore she is unable to taste danger. But there is a very big difference with Peggy; she has fairy magic and fairy speed."

"So that's the reason," said Battell. "When I first saw her speed, I couldn't quite believe it. Every spell that I sent to her, no matter how fast, I got it back, and I could hardly see her move."

Savajic went on, "I have already approached the fairy world and have asked them if they could give Peggy animal instinct, and they have said that they can. I am now waiting to hear if the Golden Fairy Queen will give them her permission."

"How has this all come about?" Battell asked.

"It's a long story, and I really have to go," Savajic said. "But I am sure that Professor Ableman will tell you what you wish to know. Now, if you will please excuse me, I must be on my way." He turned and left the room.

Professor Ableman said, "Please sit down, Battell, and I will tell you Peggy's story." When he had finished, Battell sat there quite still. He was still taking it all in.

"That's a remarkable story, Headmaster," he said. "It seems to me that we have a very special wizard in Peggy."

"Yes, we have indeed," said the professor. "Now, Battell, I want you to work on her reactions technique. Surprise her, trick her, lie to her to defeat her, try every trick in the book. But be careful with her, and explain your actions as you go along, and make sure that she understands it. Make it crystal-clear to her that everything you do to her, every trick and every trap, is exactly what she should expect from her enemies, and that they will do it and show no mercy."

"I will do my very best, Headmaster, you have my word. I can't begin to imagine what Peggy could achieve with animal instinct. I do hope that she gets permission from the Fairy Queen."

Chapter 19
SURF POLO

Peggy was studying a surf polo rule book. It wasn't anything like the polo that humans played, apart from hitting the ball with a mallet. The ball itself was round, but the core inside was offset, making it impossible to roll it true along the ground. Yet you were not allowed to strike the ball unless it was touching the ground. The mallets had an angled face, the same as a golf club, and this enabled the player to move the ball from off the ground and through the air in a straight line. The field itself was huge, and was marked with a white line running through the centre, giving the field two halves. Each half was big enough to hold four football pitches. Running from left to right in each half were two lines of holes. Each hole led directly to the opponent's half of the field, so if the attacking team hit the ball into one of the holes by mistake, the ball would travel back to their own half, and the advantage would switch to their opponent.

To score a goal, the ball had to go through the hole of a target that was made up of three rings sitting on top of each other. The bottom ring had a three-metre hole, the next one had a two-metre hole, and the one on top had a one-metre hole. Each hole had a value; 1 for the bottom, 2 for the middle, and 3 for the top hole. And last but not least were the chaos screamers; these were soft, plastic cylinders that shot up from out of the ground and burst open on contact, sending out a shower of soft and heavy screaming balls of rubber, all capable of knocking a player off their boards. As soon as they touched the ground, they disappeared. They were set in the field in a chaos pattern. There were six in each side of the field. No one knew where they were, and they were never in the same place twice.

Peggy was preparing for a house practice game; Angus had kindly let her take his place, and she was really excited. She said, "thank you, Angus," and gave him a hug and a kiss on the cheek. Angus had a big smile on his face and thought to himself, *that's a result.*

The only difference between a practice match and fixture match was the absence of chaos screamers. they were designed for total surprise, and practise with them was strictly forbidden.

The two teams had been mixed up to make the game fair. Peggy was put with Helda, Lilly, Kate and Fatima, and four boys from the form below them. Opposite was Owen, Charlie, Singh and Sal, and five girls from the form below. Angus was keeping the score.

Both teams were in a huddle, discussing tactics. Angus called the teams together, and reminded them that it was a friendly match, and he didn't want any cheating. "Now take your places."

Helda had won the toss and was standing over the ball, waiting for the whistle. Angus blew, and they were off. Helda passed the ball to Peggy on the right, and immediately went screaming up the middle of the field, followed closely by Lilly to her right. As the ball hit the ground, Peggy hit it with every ounce of power that she had, and it flew over Lilly's head and landed twenty metres in front of her. She got there first and hit it to Helda, who had arrived just as the ball touched the ground. She hit it with such force that it flew right through the top hole of the goal and disappeared.

Charlie looked at Owen and the team. "We've just been mugged," he said. "Come on, let's show them how to play." The first half was even at 7-7. And now they squared up to each other again for the second half. The whistle blew, and they were off again. The lower form players were really impressive, and they were more than holding their own, which was great news, because they were the future for Redgrave.

Thirty seconds to go and the score was 15-16 to the boys. Charlie had a big grin on his face and was getting ready to celebrate, then the grin suddenly disappeared. With the last hit of the game, Peggy smashed the ball towards the goal; she miscued and hit Helda Scelda on the head, and it ricocheted into the top hole of the goal. The whistle blew for full time and the girls had done it; they had beaten the boys 18-16. Charlie fell on the ground and looked up at the scoreboard in total disbelief, while the girls were trying to revive Helda Scelda and tell her that they had won.

That night at dinner, the word had gone all around the school. Even the teachers were aware of what had happened. All that they could get out of Charlie was how they had been robbed on the day by a pure fluke, and how it would be a different story the next time around.

Professor Ableman looked on at all the good-humoured bantering and thought to himself, *this is how it should be. This is what life should be all about.* He stroked his silver beard; if only grownup wizards could act like his pupils…but alas, he knew that it wasn't to be. The wizard world was heading into perilous times, and it would take all of their resolve to prevail. When he went back to his rooms after dinner, he found a message on the screen wall. "Good news." It was from Savajic, informing him that the Golden Fairy Queen had agreed to grant them their request and give Peggy animal instinct. He gave him the time and day when he was coming to pick Peggy up, and signed off.

The professor poured himself a glass of sherry and sat down in one of the large and well-worn leather chairs facing the fire. He sipped his drink and gazed at the flickering flames. They were almost hypnotic, and as he relaxed, his mind went back almost eighty years to his first day as headmaster of The Black Eagle School for Wizards. It had all been so different then; he was young and powerful, and held several records for wand speed and sport. And he was one of the youngest wizards ever to win a professorship. Then, at the age of forty-five years, he was appointed headmaster of The Back Eagle School for Wizards. It was the proudest day of his life.

But how times had changed. He suddenly realised how the outside world had passed him by in terms of current affairs. He knew little or nothing of the power and the reforming of the Black Watch, and worse still, the confidence that they had to reform the Death Riders. He now knew in his heart that through the Black Magic rites that they held, they had probably contacted Lord Kanzil and informed him of Baldric Zealotte's return, and he in turn would exert his power of gravity to bring the time bubble back down to Earth. Lord Kanzil had waited over a thousand years to claim the soul of Baldric Zealotte and be reunited with The Sword of Destiny; he would make sure that the time bubble would be pulled back down to Earth.

Chapter 20

ANIMAL INSTINCT

Savajic was back home in his workshop; he had taken his hologram camera to Enzebadier and Commander Churmill, and left it for them to work out a strategy and time scale for any immediate action to be taken. He had promised them that he would be on call 24/7 for their next meeting.

Suddenly there was a bright blue flash and Bluebell appeared. "Sorry if I startled you, Savajic, but I bring you good news. The Golden Fairy Queen has given her permission for us to give Peggy animal instinct, and the Silver Fairy is ready and waiting. We will need to have Peggy for a whole day, so that we can test her to the limits of her ability. Can you arrange for Peggy to be by the great oak tree in the meadow by her cottage, two days from now, and we will do the rest?"

"Yes, of course," said Savajic. "Leave it with me. She will be there waiting for you."

"Thank you," said Bluebell, and disappeared in a blue flash.

Peggy had been informed that Savajic was coming early in the morning to take her to see Bluebell. She hadn't been given a reason why, but she couldn't wait to see her. She had finished her breakfast and had gone to get changed, and now she was on her way to the headmasters rooms. She was wearing her trainers, and one of the laces had come undone. She stooped to tie it up and as she did, a flash of light passed over her and hit the wall, gouging out a large hollow. Someone was trying to kill her! And all the students and teachers were still at breakfast. She knew that she had to deal with this herself. She turned to face whoever had fired the spell at her, and she was still crouching. Then she took a deep breath and stood up. On the opposite side of the school stood a wizard, facing her, and as soon as he saw her stand up he lifted his wand.

Peggy waited for him to point it at her, then she went into action. "Flecta!" she screamed; it hit the wizard so hard that he left the ground and smashed right through one of the windows. The noise of splintering glass brought the wizards pouring out of the Great Hall from both directions to see what was happening. Peggy put her wand away and carried on to the headmaster's rooms.

She knocked on the door. "Come in," said the headmaster.

Peggy entered the room and looked at the headmaster and Savajic; she was shaking. "I'm afraid that I have just had to kill a wizard in self-defence," she said, and slumped down on one of the chairs.

Savajic said, "Killed a wizard? What do you mean?"

"I had just changed my clothes for today's trip and was on my way here; my lace had come undone. I bent down to tie it up and as I did, a spell came over me and crashed into the wall, making a hole. I was still crouching down so I turned towards where the spell had come from, and then I stood up to face whoever it was. When I saw him, I waited for him to lift his wand and point it, then I sent it back to him. I have no idea what spell he used, but whatever it was, it killed him. I had left the Great Hall early because of our trip, and everyone was still having breakfast, so I am sure no one saw me fight with the wizard."

"Do you know who it was, Peggy?"

"I'm not sure, but I think it was one of the replacement teachers from White Eagle. He's lying in one of the classrooms opposite Redgrave. I'm sorry, but the window is damaged quite badly."

"Never mind the damage to the window," said Savajic. "Are you all right?"

"I feel a bit shaky," she said, holding out her hand; it was trembling. She rubbed her hands together in an attempt to stop it.

"Sit there for a moment, Peggy, and try to relax." the professor's voice was soft and soothing. He held out his left hand and circled it with his wand, and instantly a steaming mug of hot milk appeared.

"Peggy, I would like you to stay here and sip this while Savajic and I go and investigate. Will you do that for me?"

"Yes," said Peggy, and sat back in the chair, cupping the warm mug in her hands.

When they got there, Battell Crie had taken charge. He had sent the students away, and covered the body with a blanket. "Headmaster, Savajic," he said, as they walked into the classroom. He lifted the blanket from the body.

Savajic examined the wound and said, "As I suspected; he used a death blast."

"Who did?" asked Battell.

"He did," said Savajic.

Battell looked at him with a puzzled look on his face. "He used it on himself?"

"No," said Savajic. "He tried to kill Peggy with it, but by pure luck Peggy bent down to tie the lace up on her trainer and he missed her with the first one. But when he sent the second one Peggy was ready for him and sent it back with a Flecta spell and killed him."

"Did anyone see her?" Battell asked.

"She said that she was certain that no one was around."

Battell still looked anxious. "Have you heard from the fairies yet?"

"Yes," said Savajic. "I'm taking her there now, and not a moment too soon, may I add. Headmaster, can you look after all of this? I need to get Peggy moving, and I promise you that I will come back as soon as I can."

"Yes, leave it to us. We will make up some kind of story about an experiment going badly wrong. Now you carry on," said the headmaster, "and wish Peggy good luck from us."

Bluebell was waiting for them when they arrived. Savajic apologised. "I'm sorry that we're late, but we had an incident at the school and it was unavoidable. I am sure Peggy will tell you all about it. Now please excuse me, but I must get back to Black Eagle." he held his pendant and disappeared.

Peggy followed Bluebell into the forest and they both went into a Haze. They were soon approaching the fairy camp. As they got up closer, several of the fairies greeted her by name. Peggy was amazed. "How do they know my name?" she asked Bluebell.

She smiled at Peggy and said, "Well, ever since you helped retrieve Savajic's wand from Demodus, and the valuable information that we gathered, all the fairies know who you are."

They reached the Silver Cave, and the Silver Fairy was there to greet them. "Peggy, how nice it is to see you again. Please come and sit with me, and I will explain the reason for your visit here today." Peggy had been in the Silver Cave before, but she still couldn't believe how beautiful it was. "Over here," the Silver Fairy said, and gestured to a chair.

"Now, Peggy, I realise that this must all seem very mysterious to you today, but what happens today must remain a secret that you will never divulge to any living being for as long as you live. We are going to visit the Golden Fairy Queen in Ireland, and when we arrive, she will explain in detail what today is all about." Suddenly Peggy felt excited; what can it be? She thought, *do the fairies want me to help them again?*

They were now on their way to the docking bay, and the pilot was waiting for them when they arrived. She helped the Silver Fairy into her seat, and then she helped Peggy. Then she sat in the pilot's seat and closed the canopy. One minute later she was opening it again. They were docked, and they were in Ireland.

Two of the queen's fairies were waiting for them, ready to escort the Silver Fairy and Peggy to the Golden Cave. As they came closer to the Golden Cave, Peggy could feel her heart pounding she was so excited. She could remember the last time that she had seen the Golden Fairy Queen, and how kind she had been to her.

At last they were there, and Peggy was standing in front of the queen. "Hello, Peggy, how nice it is to see you again. I hope that you are enjoying your time at Black Eagle."

"Yes, I am, Your Majesty," Peggy replied. "I have met and made lots of new friends, and I have been taught so many new things. I am very lucky and very happy. And one of the best things ever was meeting Savajic. He has been like a father to me."

"I am so pleased to hear that you are enjoying your school, Peggy, and that you have made so many new friends. We have, however, been monitoring your progress here, and unfortunately you have made many enemies as well. Not by your own making, may I add, but evil forces are at work, and you have become one of their targets.

"This brings me to the reason for your visit here today. We have been informed about the attempts on your life, and so far how you have had good fortune on your side. Unfortunately, good fortune has a tendency to run out. Savajic has informed us that you have little or no sense of danger, and because your body is human, you do not have a Calatium Gland, and therefore cannot be taught the art of tasting danger.

"Savajic came to the conclusion that the fairy world could maybe help you by giving you animal instinct. He was right, because being human, you have a natural affinity with all creatures on Earth. But because of this, we had to get permission from Mother Earth herself to grant you this; we talked together for some considerable time in order to make it as good as possible, and this is what we decided to do.

"The owl has superior hearing to most living creatures. It can pinpoint the smallest of movements in any direction, even in the dark. Coupled with a reaction time of .05 of a second, very little of its prey will ever escape.

"The bear has probably the best sense of smell of all the animal world, and is thought to be able to smell as far as two miles away, helping him to seek out food and find a mate deep in the wilderness. With a good sense of smell comes a good sense of taste, which guards against eating anything that is poisoned or contaminated.

"Birds of prey have easily the best eyesight, being able to spot a rabbit in a field from 3,000 feet in the sky, and swoop down at up to 100 miles per hour, keeping the rabbit in perfect focus all the way down. But we came to the conclusion that to have it may hinder you rather than help, so we discounted it. Human eyes have a quality of defining colour much better than most animals, and we thought that seeing and understanding colours were important. You already have 20/20 eyesight, but we can make it 20/10, the best a human has ever had, and it should not feel strange to you.

"You are going to be given one more magic power: the power to lie on the ground and draw energy from Mother Earth when you are exhausted, and the ability to pass on some of your energy to others.

"Now, Peggy, have you understood all that I have said to you," Peggy said, "Yes, Your Majesty, I have."

"Good," said the queen. "Then do you wish to accept these gifts?"

"Yes, I do," Peggy answered.

"Then we can proceed. I want you to know that these gifts come directly from Mother Earth, and not from me. You are about to be given some of the most ancient magic the world has ever known."

Chapter 21

THE GIFT

The queen led the way to the Golden Birthing Tree. When they arrived, a space had been cleared, and all the fairies had left. "Take off all your clothes and lie down on your back on the space marked next to the tree. Now put your arms down by your side and relax. Let your body feel heavy, and sink into the ground." Peggy followed the queen's instructions. The queen spoke again. "Close your eyes and go to sleep-sleep-sleep-sleep------."

Peggy slipped off into a deep sleep. She felt that she was floating in time and space. a voice came drifting faintly through the darkness of the void. "Peggy, can you hear me?"

"Yes I can hear you. Who are you?"

"Do not be afraid, for I am Mother Earth. You will not be able to see me, but you are quite safe. I am about to take you on a very special journey."

It was suddenly light, and Peggy was looking down on a very familiar scene. she was perched on the roof of the old mill down by the river in Little Thatch Village. What was going on? She thought to herself. Then the truth dawned on her; she had taken on the form of a barn owl. For a moment she panicked and called out, "Mother Earth! Can you hear me?"

"Yes, I can hear you, Peggy. Do not be alarmed; you are going to learn how to hunt using your powers of hearing and reaction."

"I don't know where to start!" Peggy said.

"And this is where you are going to learn, Peggy. I will take you over, and get you to catch several small rodents. Each time that you do, I want you to concentrate on each sound that you hear, and every movement that you make, and bank it firmly into your memory. Do you understand?"

"Yes, I can do that."

"Good then let us begin." The sun was going down, and darkness came creeping across the fields towards her. She had never experienced being in the fields at night before. It was a different world, and in a strange way, it seemed to come to life.

Whoosh! Suddenly she was in the night air, circling the fields, and her eyes were scanning the ground. Her senses were aroused, and her concentration was on full alert. She could hear a rustling noise in the grass to her left, and her head swivelled in the direction of the sound. There it was; a small field mouse, scurrying for cover. She swooped, and her talons wrapped around the little body and it was airborne all in seconds. "Fly down and let it go," the voice came softly to her, and she followed the instructions and let it go. The little mouse found a hole and disappeared.

She was perched on the roof of the old mill again and the voice spoke to her: "what did you feel, Peggy?"

"I felt the wind in my face and my wings were still. I was gliding silently across the field. Then I heard the movement of the mouse before I saw it, and my head turned to the direction of the sound and I saw it. After that there was no escape for the mouse."

"That was very good for your first attempt, now again." Five more times she went, and all in different directions. Each time she let the target go after it had been caught.

"It is now up to you, Peggy. Are you ready?"

Yes, I'm ready," she said, and took off. She had climbed high in the night sky and was gliding around in a downward spiral, her senses on full alert. She picked up a rustling noise; it was coming from the tall grass on the riverbank. she swooped down at full speed and attacked. There was a loud scream, and a large, furry arm shot out and ripped at her wing, pulling out several feathers. She let go and shot up into the air, and landed back on the old mill roof. She was badly shaken, and sat quietly thinking about what had just happened. The voice was back, speaking to her. "What lessons have you just learned, Peggy?"

She knew exactly what she had done, and she was so mad with herself. "It's a lesson that my mother taught me when I was a little girl, and I totally disregarded it without a second thought."

"And what lesson was that, Peggy?"

"Look before you leap; that lesson."

"Very good," said the voice. "Always remember to identify your target before you attack; it is not a good idea to attack large cats, one of nature's fiercest predators."

"Now, Peggy, I want five captures. And make sure that you identify your prey each time." She would not make the same mistake again, and went to work with renewed vigour. It took just under an hour to complete five more captures, and she was delighted. "Well done, Peggy. You now have the hearing and the reactions equal to that of an owl."

Peggy began to spiral back into dark space, and just as suddenly, she was back in the sunshine, somewhere deep in the Rocky Mountains. She looked up at the sky and let out a deafening roar; she had turned into a large, male grizzly bear.

The voice was back again, speaking in Peggy's mind: "I want you to concentrate on everything around you. I am going to take you on a journey through the forest and into the mountains, and on the way you will be learning how to navigate your way around, and how to find food and shelter. and you will be doing all of this purely by smell. When we reach our destination you will have a short rest, and then you must find your own way back to here by remembering all the different smells that you experienced on your way out, and without my help. Now, if you are ready, we will make a start."

Peggy found herself moving across the forest floor, and discovered how secure and balanced it felt when walking on all four paws. She was surprised at the speed she was travelling. All the time her large nostrils were taking in the different smells and analysing them; the secret, she thought, was to give each smell a picture, and to build her own index and memorise it. She was feeling hungry, and realised that she was searching for food; she knew that bears needed plenty of food, and thought to herself, *this should be interesting.* Her sense of smell was taking her towards a fast-running shallow river. Perhaps she was going to drink first, she thought, and then she saw them; salmon, swimming upstream. Suddenly she was in the water, and her powerful arms were thrashing the water. Then she felt the impact of something solid, and when she raised her arm, she could see that her long claws were imbedded in the body of a large salmon, and she was on her way back to the riverbank. As soon as she was on dry land, one paw held the salmon's head down and the other held down the tail, and she bit into its soft belly. In minutes, both sides had been devoured, and she was heading back to the river. One hour later, eight salmon carcasses lay strewn along the riverbank, and she felt quite full up. She watched, fascinated, by what was happening. Birds had appeared, and were picking at the carcasses. The ones that they had finished with were covered with ants; nothing seemed to go to waste in the forest.

She lay on the ground for about an hour, digesting the enormous amount of salmon that she had just eaten. Then she stood up stretched, and began travelling again. The cover of the forest came to an abrupt end and she was at the base of a mountain, out in the open. She could see a flock of sheep-like animals further up the mountain, but she had no idea what they were. One or two of them looked up at her and gave her an uninterested glance, and then looked away. Whatever they were, they were obviously used to seeing bears and felt no threat from them.

She stopped suddenly and stood upright, and she started sniffing the air; smoke. She could smell smoke, and animals don't light fires, so that meant that there was a human presence. She could feel an anxious sense of danger welling up inside, because humans this far up country meant hunters. She looked around for the tell-tale plume of smoke rising into the sky and there it was, over to her left. But it must have been at least a mile away. She knew that she could take nothing for granted; the hunters may have left their camp and could be heading her way.

She dropped down on all fours and took off, not stopping until she was behind the cover of the rocks further up the mountain. She had come to the mountain to check on a cave that she intended to use during the long, cold winter. One hour later, she was there. It was quite a small entrance and she squeezed her way through. Five metres in it opened out to a good-sized cave. She was amazed at how easily she had found it again. For a bear it was easy; there had been hundreds of smells and signs that had led her back there. She looked around and scratched at the floor for a while, then lay down and went to sleep.

When she awoke it was dark. "Can you hear me, Peggy?" It was Mother Earth speaking to her.

Peggy answered, "Yes, Mother Earth, I can hear you."

Good. Now your task is to go back to where we started earlier. It is dark and dangerous, so be careful. Remember the smells that you encountered on the way. You will not hear from me again until you are back to where you started. Good luck, Peggy."

Peggy left the cave behind as she started her way back down the mountain. It all looked so different in the dark. The sky was clear, and the moon cast strange-looking shadows amongst the rocks. As she moved quickly across the foot of the mountain she cast a large shadow, and was conscious that she could easily be seen if there were any hunters lurking about in the shadows. She reached the edge of the forest and felt relieved now that she was under cover. This was where her sense of smell would be truly tested, because it was pitch-black under the trees. There were hundreds of different smells, from rotting leaves on the forest floor to the sweet smell of fruit and berries. She could even pick up the scent of the nocturnal creatures scurrying around looking for food. Speaking of which, she suddenly felt hungry herself.

She had been travelling for about two hours and was making good time. She thought in another hour or so she would be back to where she had started. Hunger was really setting in now and she was ready to eat. A familiar scent came wafting in from her right; it was fresh meat. It wouldn't take her far out of her way, and she was truly hungry. She changed direction and headed for the new scent; there it was, the body of one of the sheep-like creatures that she had seen on the mountain slope. She stopped and looked around. Something had killed it, and she did not want to get into a fight with another animal whose kill it might be. She sniffed the air carefully, and no animal scent was present other than the dead body, so she edged forward towards the body. *Snap!* Pain shot up her leg. She had stepped into a bear trap, and its vicious teeth bit into her flesh. She had made a stupid mistake and let her hunger cloud her judgement. For an instant, her memory took her back to her time with Owen in the stone maze; *patience, Peggy, patience.* He had captured her twice because she couldn't wait. And now she was trapped, all because she couldn't wait one more hour to get back and have all the salmon she could eat.

Fortunately for her, Peggy was a bear with a human brain. Instead of panicking and trying to break free she stood quite still, and tried to reason the situation through. Firstly, the trap would have to be anchored to something, so it would probably be staked to the ground, in which case with her strength, she could pull the stakes out one at a time. Then again, with her strength she could simply pry it open, something a bear would never think of doing. She pushed a paw down in between the teeth of the trap in front of her massive leg, and her other paw down behind her leg, and with a mighty heave, opened the trap and freed her leg. *I must get back*, she thought. Then she stopped and looked down at the trap. It was an evil-looking thing. "Let's have some sport," she said to herself. She bent down and heaved at the trap until it clicked open. She carefully positioned it back to where it had originally been and stood up. She reached out and picked up the dead animal and dropped it into the trap; it snapped shut. *That will give the trappers something to think about in the morning,* she thought as she headed back.

She was back at last, and her leg had completely healed. "Very good," said a voice in her head. "You have done well, Peggy, and you coped confidently with the challenge that I set for you on the way back. Had you shown a little more patience, you would not have needed to escape. But now it is time to get you back and leave this poor bear in peace. You have proved to me that you are capable of using your new instincts. All that I ask of you is that you use them carefully, and show more patience."

Peggy's eyes opened and she looked up at the Golden Birthing Tree. It was beautiful. she was back. "Ah, Peggy! You're awake!" it was a fairy, holding her clothes. "Please get dressed, and I will take you to the queen." Peggy dressed and followed closely behind the fairy on her way to see the queen; she had no idea how long she had been away, but she guessed that it was probably most of the day.

The queen greeted Peggy with a wonderful smile. "Well done, Peggy. Mother Earth has spoken well of you, and expressed how pleased she was with your progress. Now, Peggy, could I have your thoughts on your trip with Mother Earth?"

"It was wonderful, Your Majesty, and nothing like I could ever have imagined it to be. I actually became an owl, so that I could learn how to hear and react like one. But all the time it was me in an owl's body. I felt how it was to fly, and at the same time pick up the smallest of sounds and hone in and capture small creatures. And I re-learned an old lesson to look before I leap.

"Then I became a bear so that I could learn how to smell my way around in the forest, with its hundreds of different scents. and I learned how to smell danger; and I even went fishing and caught some salmon. And all the time that I was a bear I felt that it was me. Mother Earth gave me one more lesson, a painful one, and one that I will remember: the virtue of patience. The chance to become an owl and a bear was unbelievable, and I will never, ever forget the experience."

The queen held Peggy's hands. "Mother Nature gave you much more than you think she did, Peggy. You need to understand that to use your new powers, you have to become as one with the creature whose instincts you wish to use."

"I don't understand what you mean, Your Majesty," Peggy said, feeling embarrassed.

"Let me explain it to you," the queen said. If you look carefully at an owl, you will notice that it has a flat face with large eyes, and ears both pointing directly in front. This enables it to pick up the smallest of sounds, and an ability to see quite well in the dark. It also has another very clever trick up its sleeve; it can swivel its head 180 degrees in both directions, giving it the ability to see in a complete circle.

"The bear has a very long nose, with waves of skin running the whole length in each nostril. Each wave of skin carries thousands of sensors, giving the bear one of the most powerful senses of smell on Earth. and with exceptional smell comes exceptional taste. Unfortunately, the human body has none of these characteristics, and so to use them you have to become as one with the creature."

Peggy looked at the queen, perplexed, and said to her, "well, unless I can change into an owl or a bear then I can't use my new powers?"

"That is correct," the queen replied. "Peggy, Mother Earth has given you much more magic than you think she has. She has given you the power to transfigure."

"You mean that I can change into a bear?" she said in disbelief.

"That's exactly what I mean. Take a step back, close your eyes, and think that you are a bear." Peggy took a step back, closed her eyes and said to herself, *I am a bear*. She opened her eyes, and she was a bear. "Now can you understand what I mean?" the queen said, smiling at Peggy and thinking how well she had done.

Peggy closed her eyes and said, "I'm Peggy Goody," and she was back to herself again.

The queen said, "Now, there is something else. You need to know that you can transfigure into any bear. Close your eyes and say, 'I am a polar bear'." Peggy did as the queen asked, and suddenly there was an ear-splitting roar. When she opened her eyes she was a polar bear, and was towering some three metres tall over the queen. She quickly changed back, afraid that she may have frightened the queen.

The queen was smiling at her. "The same rules apply to the owl inasmuch as you can transfigure into any species of bird. Mother Earth has given you one more gift; the power to recharge your energy and share it by touching. Until today, only the fairy world has had this ability, so you are very fortunate, and I hope that you use it well.

"The hard work begins now, Peggy, and like everything else, you need to practice as much as possible. Much of your new powers will transfer to your human body, but not all, so always be ready to transfigure when possible. I want you to go back to Black Eagle now and carry on with your studies, and remember; only the wizards that need to know will know of your powers, so tell no one at all. This will be your secret weapon. Now it is time for you to leave. May good fortune be with you, Peggy. Good-bye."

When the Silver Fairy and Peggy arrived at the docking area, the pilot was waiting for them. She helped them into the shuttle; a minute later they were alighting at the Silver Cave. Bluebell was waiting for them, and bowed to the Silver Fairy and gave Peggy a hug; a hug that said so much for the feelings they had for each other. The Silver Fairy and Peggy exchanged their farewells, and Bluebell began leading the way back to the great oak tree. When they arrived, Savajic was there waiting.

Peggy ran to him and threw her arms around him; it was the gesture of a daughter to her father. She didn't say a word, she just hugged him. Their bond seemed unbreakable. Bluebell broke the silence. "I must leave you now," she said. "Good fortune be with you, Peggy, and remember; practice-practice-practice." There was a blue flash, and she was gone.

Savajic was beaming at Peggy. "How did you go?" he asked.

"Oh! It was unbelievable," she said, and she didn't stop talking all the way back to Black Eagle.

They made straight for the headmaster's room. "Please come in and sit down." the professor gestured towards two chairs. As soon as they were seated, the professor looked at Peggy and said, "I believe that congratulations are in order. Well done, Peggy. Now then, let me hear of your progress. Did you grasp all that was taught to you?"

"I did," Peggy answered, "but the Golden Fairy Queen has given me strict instructions not to tell anyone of my new powers, because she said that it will give me a secret weapon."

"It's all right, Peggy," Savajic said. "The headmaster, Enzebadier the Elder, you, and myself all know of your new powers, but you are quite right; no one else must find out; not even Owen."

Peggy spent the next hour going over her experiences as an owl and a bear, and showed them how she could transfigure. They were very impressed with her. Savajic told her that there were some wizards that could transfigure, and almost all of them by Black Magic; but he knew of no other wizard that could transfigure into several different creatures like she could. He added, "I feel so much better now I know that you will be able to sense danger more easily."

The Headmaster stood up and stretched. "I think that we all need a good night's sleep. It has been quite a day. Peggy, tomorrow it's back to normal, if that is possible." She was feeling tired and was glad to be excused. She headed for a hot shower and an early night.

Chapter 22
Fu-Jin-Mojo

Peggy was on her way to the gym for a lesson with Professor Crie. For the last three weeks he had been working her as hard as he could, and since her visit to see Mother Earth, she was proving to be quite a handful for him to manage. As she walked through the door she was immediately hit by the smell of incense, and sitting cross-legged in middle of the gym was what looked like a Chinese priest.

"Come in, Peggy, and meet Fu-Jin-Mojo!" boomed Professor Crie. The Chinese priest stood up with remarkable agility and walked towards her. She carefully watched his every move, ready to make a move of her own. For the last three weeks Professor Crie had tried everything in the book, and then some, to try and trick her and render her at a disadvantage, so she was taking no chances, especially with a total stranger.

"Please relax, Peggy." the voice was high-pitched, but soothing. "I am here to help you with your lessons. I wish you no harm. I can sense your apprehension. Please let me introduce myself; I am Fu-Jin-Mojo, a Kando Grand Master, and I am from the Tiger Temple, high in the White Mountains in northern China. Enzebadier contacted me and asked me if I would come to Black Eagle and teach you the ancient art of Kando.

"Kando is the art of dislocation; wrists, arms, legs, shoulders, and all other joints. The purpose is to render an enemy defenceless without taking a life, but if there is no other alternative, we have six strikes, all killers. I have been invited to stay at Black Eagle for three weeks so that I can give you lessons in between your other activities."

Peggy had relaxed, and greeted him. "Thank you for giving me the opportunity to learn your ancient secrets, Grand Master." she took his hand and held his gaze, they both bowed to each other, then stepped away.

"Please sit with me, Peggy." They both sat down on the gym floor and crossed their legs. For our first lesson, I just want to talk about you; yourself, and your future say in five years' time. I have talked at length with Savajic, and he thinks that some time in the future you will go back and live in the human world, and possibly work for the British government. If this is so then I must warn you, that you will not be the only one to possess the skills of Kando. There is one other temple that teaches this knowledge, and they are not all good students. Over the years there have been defectors who have travelled the world, selling their skills to the highest bidder. Some have worked as assassins for many bad people. I am sure from what Savajic has told me that you will probably handle most things that come your way, but to be forewarned is to be forearmed.

"I believe that you posses great strength, so we have to be careful how we practice, and only total concentration will do. I have also been informed by the headmaster that our lessons are to be kept a secret, so it will be better if you will pretend that you are having lessons with Professor Crie, who will be present at all of the lessons. Now, Peggy, I look forward to our next lesson."

The next three weeks were solid work for Peggy. When it was time for Grand Master Fu-Jin-Mojo to leave, she was genuinely upset to see him go, because they had forged a close friendship and a mutual respect for each other. Through his great skill as a teacher, Peggy had added another awesome string to her bow.

When Grand Master Fu-Jin-Mojo had arrived at Black Eagle three weeks earlier he had caused quite a stir, because he had arrived on a Chinese Red Dragon, a very rare and sacred creature. His departure was going to be the same; the dragon was tethered in the grounds at the back of the Great Hall, and most of the students and teachers were there to see him off. As they rose into the air, an ear-splitting cheer rang out. He waved to them, and disappeared through the massive castle doors. Peggy had been watching through the headmaster's window that overlooked the grounds and when he was gone, she sat down. In the room was the headmaster, Battell Crie, Savajic, and herself.

The headmaster began, "the Grand Master was very pleased with your progress, Peggy, and complimented me on the school itself and for the high standard of our pupils. Battell, would you like to comment on Peggy's progress?"

"Yes I would, Headmaster. Peggy has worked extremely hard in everything that we have done together, and since her visit to the Fairy World, her instincts have become razor-sharp. I can no longer out-manoeuvre her, and I believe that as she practices, she will be even better. I think that Peggy should spend a period of time on her own in the forest and practice her skills with the creatures around her; a survival period, with no help from the school."

"Do you think that it is wise?" asked the Headmaster, considering what had transpired since the new term began. "What do you think, Peggy?"

"I don't have any objections to a period in the forest; it would give me plenty of time to do things without having to answer questions all the time. Having said that, I would welcome a few weeks first with my friends, to do a bit of catching up, and then perhaps fit it in before the Christmas holidays."

"Very well then," said the headmaster. "I will leave that in your capable hands; Battell, will you get it organised?"

"Yes of course, Headmaster."

Savajic was the next to speak. "As you know, I will busy with the War Council, and almost all of my time will be taken up with this. So unless you have need of me, I will not be back to Black Eagle for the foreseeable future. Peggy, before I go, a word of caution; pay attention to detail. Keep your wand safe, and trust no one at face value."

Peggy stood up and crossed the room. She held out her hands, and Savajic gripped them. Then she looked into his eyes and said, "Please be careful."

"I will," he said, and then he left.

Chapter 23

BAD NEWS FROM AMERICA

When Peggy got back to the girls' room, they were all grouped around Kate's bed. She was sitting there crying, and Lilly was sitting next to her with her arm around her. "What's happened?" asked Peggy. "Has she had an accident?"

"No," said Helda. "I'm afraid she's had some bad news from home. Her father has been taken ill." Peggy knew that Kate's father had been frail for some years; he had never quite got over losing Kate's mother in a riding accident.

Peggy moved in close to Kate and bent down and whispered in her ear, "I think that I might be able to help your father, but we must leave right away."

Kate looked up at her and said, "What do you mean?"

Peggy held out her hand and said, "Come with me to the headmaster's rooms, now." it almost sounded like a command, and they all looked at her in amazement. Kate shot to her feet and grabbed Peggy's hand and they started for the headmaster's rooms. They moved in silence, not wanting to speak until they got there.

As they approached the headmaster's room the door swung open and a voice said, "Whatever is the matter, Peggy?"

"Have you heard of Kate's bad news yet?"

"No," said the headmaster. "What bad news?"

"Kate's father has been taken seriously ill in America, and I think that I can help him, but we need to go now. You are aware of my power to give energy, and I think that it will aid his recovery."

The headmaster turned to the wall. "Screen," he ordered, and the wall changed immediately. "Enzebadier," he commanded, and Enzebadier appeared.

"Headmaster, how can I be of assistance to you?" he asked. "I see you have Peggy with you; greetings."

"I need your help to transport Peggy and Kate Stringer to America right away, if possible."

Enzebadier said, "Peggy, Kate, go immediately to the terrace and you will find a military capsule waiting for you. Give the pilot your instructions, and he will take you wherever you want to go." He wished them good luck, and the screen faded.

There was no time to pack. They both ran to the terrace. When they arrived the capsule was there, and the pilot was waiting for their instructions. They were on their way, and it would take four minutes. They were aboard the latest military fast-response capsule that travelled at non-gravitational Pulshe speed.

As soon as they touched down, they ran to the ranch house and climbed the stairs two at a time. they entered Kate's father's room and crossed over to his bedside. A wizard doctor was there doing what he could, and when he saw them he looked puzzled. "I've come to help," said Peggy. "Please, will you let me try?"

"Anything that you can do to help would be most welcome," said the doctor.

Peggy reached out and held Mr. Stringer's hands in hers. She closed her eyes and concentrated on her energy memory; *share, share, shhhhhhare.* Her body was trembling, but she held on tight. For five whole minutes she stood motionless, her energy draining from her body and transferring into Kate's father. She let go and slumped to the floor.

"Peggy!" screamed Kate, and ran to her side.

"Help me to get outside. I need to lay on the ground." Her voice was just a whisper. Kate put her arm around her and helped her down the stairs and outside and lay Peggy down on the ground. Kate was sobbing. She looked down at Peggy; she was lying there, motionless, and Kate knew that she was looking at a true and special friend. She didn't understand what Peggy had tried to do, but she knew that she had given a part of herself to her father, and given him the chance to live a little bit longer.

Peggy opened her eyes and looked up at Kate. "I'm OK, I just need to lay here for a few minutes. Please, go and check up on your father." Kate disappeared into the house, and Peggy closed her eyes and laid back. Her mind drifted off into space and a voice spoke to her.

"You have used my gift well, Peggy. Your thinking was clear and quick; well done. But a word of caution; this power will only work on the living. Never attempt to revive the dead; that power belongs to Gasieus alone." The voice faded, and Peggy opened her eyes and stood up; all her energy had returned.

Kate was hugging her father when Peggy walked into the bedroom, and there were big smiles on everyone's face. Kate saw her and ran over to her and hugged her. "Thank you, thank you, thank you! I don't know what you did, but just look at my father!" he was sitting up and wide eyed.

"Kate, listen to me carefully. What has taken place here today must remain here, I want your promise on that."

"You have it, Peggy I promise."

"Thank you," said Peggy.

"You're thanking me? You must be joking," said Kate. "You've just given me my father back."

"I haven't cured him, Kate, but I have given him the strength to fight his illness. It is now up to him and the doctor."

Peggy was ready to go back and had said her good-byes. As she stepped into the capsule she looked back and waved to Kate, and wondered if she would ever see her again. The capsule landed back on the terrace of Black Eagle, and Peggy thanked the pilot for his help. Then she started to make her way to the headmaster's rooms.

As she approached, the door opened. "Come in, Peggy, and sit down," said the headmaster. "How was your journey?"

"Very productive, I think," said Peggy. "We got there in time to help Mr Stringer, and I was able to give him quite a large amount of energy to help him fight against his illness. However, I am not sure how long it will be before we see Kate again, because obviously she will want to stay at home and look after her father until he has recovered."

The headmaster sat quietly stroking his beard, and then he said, "What made you think that you could help Kate's father?"

"I don't really know, it just came into my head that if we acted quickly enough, I might be able to give him enough of my strength to fight his illness. I don't even know what his illness is."

"I can tell you this much, Peggy; ever since Kate's mother died, her father seemed to give up on life. They were very close and he loved her dearly, and when Kate came to Black Eagle, his loneliness became unbearable. He was not suffering from a disease, he was dying of a broken heart. What you did today was to give him the strength to carry on, and realize that he has a life to live with his wonderful daughter. You did well today, Peggy; you did very well indeed."

Chapter 24

LOVE IS IN THE AIR

I t was a thousand questions when Peggy got back to the girls; if, how, what, where; it was relentless. Peggy hated to tell lies, but because of all that was going on around her she was becoming quite an accomplished liar, like it or not.

After dinner, Peggy and Charlie went for a walk on the terrace. The great gate was kept open until 9.00 p.m. each night, as a privilege for the final-year students, and was a popular place to go and get some peace and quiet and reflect on their day. They walked over to the balcony and looked down into the valley below; dusk was beginning to fall, and the first lights began twinkling in the darkness. The stars were lighting up the sky. Charlie was laughing and joking as he usually did, and then suddenly, without any warning, he spun Peggy around to face him, pulled her close, and kissed her on the lips. Peggy's surprise lasted less than a second. Her arms wrapped around Charlie and they stood there, locked in a lover's embrace.

When they parted, Charlie began to ramble on. "I'm sorry, Peggy, but you know that I'm rubbish with words, and I had to let you know how I feel. I just hope that I haven't gone and spoiled it between us." Peggy's head was spinning. She thought the world of Charlie, she always had; but this was on another level, and she liked it. she moved in close and kissed him right back.

"We have to talk about many things," said Peggy. "You have to know that I will be doing a lot of things that I can't talk to you about, and you must promise me that you will never ask. It's the only way that we can be more than just good friends."

Charlie held her and said, "I know that you will always have a secret life, and I know that you will face danger. I want to be there for you when you need someone to love and comfort you. Please, at least let's give it a try." Peggy gave him his answer with a kiss.

Chapter 25

A LETTER FROM KATE

Peggy was feeling great; a week had gone by since Charlie had told her of his feelings for her, and all the awkwardness of their relationship had disappeared. It was good—really good.

"Post!" Owen handed her two letters; one from her mother, and one from Kate. She tore open the one from Kate, hoping it would contain good news; it did. In it, Kate said that her father was a new man, and was running the ranch with renewed vigour. They had been out riding together and she said that it had made her realise how much she had missed it. She put, "Peggy, I'm not coming back. I'm going to stay here and help my father. I'm going to miss y'all terribly, and especially you, Peggy. I will never forget what you did for my father. Please do one more thing for me; take my place in the polo team and win the championship for Redgrave, then go on and beat White Eagle for the cup and stick it to the Belbur Twins.

All my love, good-bye. Kate."

It upset Peggy, and she couldn't hold back the tears. "What's up?" asked Owen. Peggy couldn't speak. She handed him the letter. He read it and said, "What a shame. Please say that you will join the team. You certainly have my blessing. Let's do it for Kate."

"You bet I will. There is no way that we're going to lose." she looked at Owen and there was fire in her eyes. They both shouted: "Yes!" and gave each other a high five.

Peggy opened the letter from her mother and got another nice surprise. Savajic had invited them both to spend the Christmas holiday at his home, and she was delighted; so was Owen when she told him.

Chapter 26

POLO + THE SCREAMERS

Owen had conveyed Kate's wishes that Peggy take her place in the Redgrave Polo team, and the team were delighted. Helda Scelda was the first to congratulate her. "You will be playing on my right!" she gushed. They were becoming really close friends since Peggy had joined her swimming team and become her number one. Helda put her arm on Peggy's shoulder and began to give her some advice about the match against the Lister team. "Three of their players are on the school team, and they are our biggest challenge this year, so we have to be on our top game to beat them. Now, you haven't played a game with Screamers, so I need to warn you that if you set one off, move away as quickly as you can. Forget about the ball, just get clear."

"I'll try and remember," said Peggy.

"Well if you don't, you will definitely remember the next time," said Helda, and gave her a squeeze.

It was match day, and the teams were dressed in their house colours; Redgrave was dressed in their red team colours, and Lister was dressed in their green team colours. Peggy had had her board painted red to match up with the rest of the team and they were all ready to go.

Benjamin Fuller, the Lister captain, started the game with the first hit. The pace was fast and furious, and the first score went to Lister; a clean shot through the centre hole, 2-0. Charlie looked over at Owen and gave some sort of signal, and he took off down the right. The ball went to Helda. She hit it to Fatima, who hit it to Peggy. Her reaction was amazing. The ball hardly touched the ground and her mallet crashed the ball through the top hole, 2-3. The students were screaming for each other's teams so loudly that they could hardly hear each other's instructions. Then Peggy encountered her first Screamer. She sensed it coming, and shot off at top speed. She just managed to get out of the way of a rubber pad coming her way; however, there was no such luck for the Lister player who was shadowing her. A rubber pad hit him square in the chest and sent him spinning off his board. He lay on the ground for a few seconds, then got up and shook his head and climbed back on his board, ready to go again.

Peggy soon realised that team games were different to the practice games. She had been bungled off her board three times and it was still in the first half of the game. *Time to toughen up,* she thought, and went full pelt at a Lister player who was just about to shoot. *Crunch!* She hit him so hard he landed on the ground, unconscious. A loud horn sounded, and the game was stopped. Peggy felt terrible; she hadn't meant to hurt him. But in one unthinking moment she had forgotten the tremendous strength that she possessed.

Professor Crie landed next to the boy and turned him onto his back. It was the captain, Benjamin Fuller. Battell glared at Peggy. "That was stupid," he growled at her. "Where's your self-control?" Then he picked up the boy and flew off towards the hospital wing.

The game was called off and the match was to be rescheduled. The crowd made their way back to the dorms, and Peggy felt isolated. Suddenly there was an arm around her and the cheerful voice of Charlie. "Come on, sport. We all know that you didn't mean to hurt him." The problem was that *she* knew that she had meant to do it. She was changing—her senses, her way of thinking—she was no longer an ordinary girl. There had been too many adult skills taught to her, and she was well in advance of her true age.

Peggy made up her mind right there and then that Black Eagle was not for her. She looked up at Charlie. He was smiling at her. She loved him, but she knew that there could never be a future for them. She said, "Charlie, I've got to go and see the headmaster. Can we catch up at dinner tonight?"

"OK, if you're sure," he said.

"I'm sure," she answered, and started walking towards the Great Hall.

Chapter 27

THE DECISION

P eggy sat opposite the headmaster and told him of her decision. "Is there nothing that I can do to make you change your mind?"

"There is nothing left for me here," she said. "I can't enter for any of the championship trophies; it wouldn't be fair. I had a sharp lesson today, and that was that it will be increasingly hard for me to hold back on my full powers. I want to go and help Savajic. I believe that somehow I have a destiny to fulfil with him, and I am sure that I can help him in the impending Hobgoblin War."

The headmaster stood up. "Very well, Peggy. Go and enjoy your dinner. I will contact Savajic and ask him if he will come here after breakfast tomorrow."

"You're quiet tonight," said Owen. "Are you still upset about the polo match?"

Peggy was playing with her food; she wasn't really hungry. "I'm sorry that I hurt Benjamin, of course, but I'm over it now, honestly. Owen, can you round the team up and meet me in the den at 9.30 tonight?"

"Yes, no problem," he said. "What's happening?"

"I'll tell you tonight in the den. I have to do something first."

Charlie was looking at her. he was concerned that something had happened when she had gone to see the headmaster. Peggy could see that he was about to start asking her questions, so before he could start she said to him, "Finish your meal, and after we can go for a walk on the terrace."

Everyone at the table was unusually quiet for a change. The air was charged, and they didn't know why. Owen stood up and tapped his glass. They stopped talking and looked his way. "Will all of you on the Redgrave team meet up with me in the den at 9.30 p.m.? Thank you." As he sat down the table cleared, signalling the end of dinner.

Peggy and Charlie walked through the gates and onto the terrace. Her heart was beating like it was ready to burst. What was she going to say to Charlie? How could she tell him that they were over even before they had really begun? As they leaned against the balustrade and looked down over the valley, Peggy was desperately trying to unscramble her thoughts, when Charlie suddenly said, "it's over between us, isn't it?" Peggy flung her arms around him and began to sob. "I guess I have my answer," he said, and felt that he had just been gutted.

Peggy looked up. "Kiss me," she begged. Charlie's arms encircled her and their lips met in a passionate embrace, an embrace that neither wanted to end.

As they parted, Charlie said, "why Peggy? Why?" His voice was soft and full of hurt, and she had a terrible feeling of guilt.

"It isn't anything that you've done; it's me, all me!" she blurted out. "I need to try and explain something to you. While we were playing polo, something unexpected happened to me. Something changed in my head, and I was no longer the person that I was when I had started playing. I hate to admit this to you, but I purposely tried to hurt Benjamin."

"I don't believe it," Charlie said, looking at her with shock written on his face. "It isn't in you."

"There is so much that I would like to tell you about but I can't. But I will tell you this much, and you must never tell anyone, not even Owen. I have the power to beat Professor Battell Crie with one arm tied behind my back, and my powers are increasing all the time. but so is my appetite to fight. This makes it very dangerous for me to take part in anything competitive. you saw today what happens when I use my strength.

"When I went to see the headmaster, I told him that I was going to leave Black Eagle, and gave him my reasons. He has given me his permission, but he stressed that he would leave the door open for me should I change my mind."

"But what will you do?" Charlie asked in a concerned voice.

"I can't tell you that because I'm not quite sure myself yet."

"Is this what the meeting in the den is all about?"

"Yes, it is, but you had to be the first to know. We needed to have this time on our own before I announced it to the rest of the team. No one but you I. And of course the headmaster, knows that I am leaving."

"Thank you for telling me this way, Peggy, but I will never stop loving you, I want you to know that."

"Charlie, I love you more than I can say, and parting like this is breaking my heart. But I know that if we carried on that I would eventually hurt you. I can tell you this; there will never be anyone but you. I will never let anyone get this close to me again."

Charlie took a deep breath. "Come on, sport. You've got a meeting to attend."

Chapter 28

TIME TO SAY GOOD-BYE

The meeting in the den was in turmoil when Peggy announced that she was leaving Black Eagle, not knowing if she would ever return. Owen was in a state of shock. "I thought that you liked it here!" he protested.

"I do," said Peggy. "I love it and everyone here, but I have no choice. I'm sorry, but I can't tell you why."

Owen spun round on Charlie. "You must know why she's leaving," he said.

"I don't," lied Charlie. "I'm just as much in the dark as you are."

Helda Scelda was beside herself. "You cannot leave us like this! You are my closest friend."

"And you, too, will always be close to my heart," said Peggy. One by one Peggy hugged the team; the meeting had been held, and the deed was done. There was nothing else to say, and they left the den in silence.

Breakfast was an awkward affair, with no one really saying much, and they were all glad to see it over and done with. They all made their way to their various classes, and Peggy made her way to the headmaster's room. The door opened and the headmaster said, "Please come in, Peggy, and sit down." She sat down facing the desk. "Have you had any second thoughts, Peggy?" the headmaster asked.

"No, Headmaster, I have not changed my mind," she said.

The door opened behind Peggy and Savajic walked in. "Thank you for coming," the headmaster said. "Please take a seat."

He sat down and said, "What's going on? Has there been another attempt to injure Peggy?"

"No, nothing like that. But a surprise nonetheless; Peggy has asked my permission to leave Black Eagle, and I have agreed.

Savajic gasped. "You want to leave Black Eagle? Why?"

Peggy stood up. "I want to show you both something." She transfigured into a Polar bear, then into a Grizzly bear, then into a Panda bear, then into a Koala bear, and then she disappeared altogether. Ten seconds later she was back as herself. Then she transfigured again, this time into an eagle, then into a vulture, then into an owl, and finally a lightning hawk. When she returned to herself she was met by a stunned silence.

"When did you realise that you could do all of this?" Savajic asked.

"Mother Earth told me in a dream that I could change into any bear or any bird that I chose to be; but as I began to practice, I realised that I still had all my brain power and control no matter what form I took. This on its own is not a problem, but I have learned to kill with my wand and with my bare hands. Professor Battell Crie will tell you that he can no longer challenge me, and Grand Master Fu-Jin-Mojo warned me that I would have to show great restraint with what he had taught me.

"In the polo match with Lister, I started off having fun. But after being purposely knocked off my board three times I felt that it was payback time. I went after Lister's captain, Benjamin Fuller, and hit him so hard he is in hospital. When I saw the way that Professor Crie looked at me, I realised that a different Peggy Goody had been born; a Peggy Goody that did not belong in a school with vulnerable pupils.

"Savajic, I want you to give me a chance to work with you in defeating Baldric Zealotte and the Hobgoblins. I know that I'm ready to take up the challenge and be useful to the wizard cause."

Savajic stood up and put his hands on Peggy's shoulders, looked her in the eyes and said, "Is this truly what you want? Are you sure?"

"I've never been more certain of anything," she said.

"Very well then, consider it done. Are you packed?"

"Yes, I am," she said.

"Then I suggest that we leave right away, with the minimum amount of fuss."

"I agree," said the headmaster. "I will tell all who need to know. Leave it to me."

"I will keep in touch with you, Headmaster," said Savajic. He turned to Peggy and said, "Let's go."

The end.